Keely didn't min
—but was this h

The man was disturbing
with his back to the roo
to the harbour below. Yes, there was something
familiar about the way he tilted his head, something
that caused Keely's blood to dance in her veins.

He was tall and lean. She could see how the
expensive cut of his charcoal suit enhanced his broad,
powerful shoulders. His carefully styled hair was the
rich colour of pecan shells and feathered the top of
his collar. This man was sleek and elegant. Powerful
and alarming.

Then the stranger turned slowly and pinned Keely
with his blue-grey eyes.

Her heart stopped.

It couldn't be... Noah Bannister, her old love, had
returned to San Diego.

And promptly, Keely reached out and slapped him
smartly across the face.

Dear Reader:

We are delighted to bring you this daring series from Silhouette®.

Intrigue™—where resourceful, beautiful women flirt with danger and risk everything for irresistible, often treacherous men.

Intrigue—where the stories are full of heart-stopping suspense and mystery lurks around every corner.

You won't be able to resist Intrigue's exciting mix of danger, deception…and desire.

Please write and let us know what you think of our selection of Intrigue novels. We'd like to hear from you.

Jane Nicholls
Silhouette Books
PO Box 236
Thornton Road
Croydon
Surrey
CR9 3RU

Undercover Vows

JUDI LIND

SILHOUETTE

Intrigue

*Silhouette and Colophon are registered trademarks of
Harlequin Books S.A., used under licence.*

*First published in Great Britain 1997
Silhouette Books, Eton House, 18-24 Paradise Road,
Richmond, Surrey TW9 1SR*

© Judith A. Lind 1996

ISBN 0 373 22355 2

46-9701

*Printed and bound in Great Britain
by Mackays of Chatham PLC, Chatham*

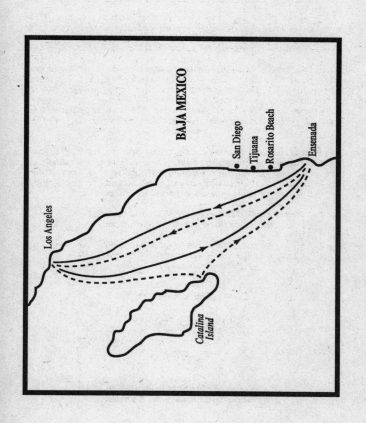

"This story is about sisters, and mine is the best.
For Jackie George, with all my love."

Chapter One

Keely Travers slowly climbed out of her car and ran her fingertips through her thick crop of short black hair. Opening the trunk, she picked up a stack of un-assembled cardboard cartons and balanced them against her hip. The boxes were heavy but Keely didn't put them down. She leaned against the car and stared at the tiny frame house that had belonged to her sister, Rosie. At least, it had been her sister's home until three days ago. The day they found Rosie's body in a crumpled Mercedes at the bottom of a canyon.

The second shock had been learning that Rosie hadn't died alone. Another body recovered at the crash site was that of a local loan shark named Marty Sargent. The newspapers hadn't been subtle in their speculations that Rosie had been entangled in some nefarious scheme with the well-known shyster.

Keely didn't believe it. She couldn't accept the possibility that her fun-loving, irrepressible sister had gotten involved in something illegal. Still, she had no answer for the nagging question of exactly why Rosie had been in the car with the loan shark in the first place.

Oh, Rosie, what happened? Keely blinked to dispel the tears that were once again pooling in her eyes. She had to stop it. This wasn't the time to dwell on the unsavory circumstances of Rosie's death. Right now she had to be strong. For Pop. And for Rosie's grieving husband, Todd.

Stiffening her shoulders against a fresh onslaught of grief, Keely tightened her arms around the cartons and took a halting step forward. *Don't think, don't feel. Just keep moving.*

By the time she reached the front door, the tough outer shell she always wore was firmly in place. San Diego PD Detective Keely Travers was once more in control. At least, that's what she kept telling herself as she unlocked the door and stepped into the dim interior.

"Here, let me help you with that!" Her brother-in-law, Todd Bannister, rushed into the living room, a white towel draped across his bare shoulders.

"Oh, thanks," she breathed as she released the clumsy bundle into his arms. "I didn't expect you to be home—I mean, I...." Her voice trailed off, leaving the half-finished indictment dangling in the air.

Todd had called her the previous evening, crying that every time he saw Rosie's clothes next to his in the closet, it was like losing her all over again. He'd begged Keely to sort through Rosie's things and, of course, she'd agreed. She always agreed. Rosie and Todd Bannister had been two of a kind—beautiful, irresponsible adult children with the enviable ability to induce others to clean up after them. Rosie and Todd had lived in a Peter Pan world where neither had ever grown up. And Keely felt as much to blame as anyone for indulging them.

Todd leaned the boxes against the back of the sofa and pulled on a rumpled shirt. Tossing the towel on the arm of a nearby easy chair, he said, "I really appreciate your doing this for me. I, uh, just can't seem to do anything without Rosie."

Keely patted his arm. Dear sweet Todd. He'd always been too gentle spirited for the harshness of life.

He pulled his car keys out of his jeans pocket and strode to the still-open front door. Pausing, he turned to face Keely. "It just isn't right. I mean, it wasn't supposed to be like this. Remember when we were kids? We were all supposed to be together. Me and Rosie, you and Noah. Forever."

Noah. Forever. The words slammed in her chest like brutal physical blows. "Oh, God, Todd, please don't start talking about Noah. Not now." Keely knew her already-battered emotions couldn't take another pummeling. The absolute last thing she needed right now was to dredge up the memory of Noah Bannister and his defection. Determined to banish the bittersweet recollection before it took hold, Keely stepped to the door and planted her palm against Todd's back, urging him out the door. "You go on now, I'll take care of this."

Planting a soft kiss on the top of her head, he murmured, "Thanks, sis. I'll be at my mom's if you need me."

She stood and watched her brother-in-law stroll down the driveway until he roared off in the beat-up Toyota pickup that had been parked at the curb. With a sigh of relief, she turned back to the empty house.

A stale musty odor permeated the room. If she knew Todd, he probably hadn't aired the house since the accident. Leaving the door propped open, Keely

crossed to the window and drew back the heavy drap-
eries and opened the sash, letting the late-afternoon
sunlight filter in. The brightness did little to dispel the
gloomy atmosphere.

An unemptied ashtray was overflowing on the coffee table, next to a desiccated, half-eaten pizza. Three
days' newspapers were discarded in front of the sofa.

Grateful for something constructive to occupy her
time, Keely rolled back the sleeves of her thin jersey
top and started gathering dirty dishes. For the next
hour her mind was blissfully numb as she plunged into
the housework.

She dusted, vacuumed, scraped dried food off the
dishes and scrubbed the kitchen floor. At last there
was nothing more to distract her, and Keely knew she
had to face the unpleasant task that awaited her. She
had to clear Rosie's things out of the bedroom.

Well, this would be the last thing she could ever do
for her sister. Blowing a lock of hair from her eyes, she
lugged the awkward cartons into the bedroom. Mind-
lessly she began boxing her sister's belongings. First
she emptied the dresser, then cleared Rosie's toiletries
off the top. Then she moved to the closet and hauled
out Rosie's incredibly gaudy wardrobe. And shoes!
Good grief, how many pairs of shoes could one
woman wear?

Rosie and Todd were forever behind in the rent, but
apparently they'd had plenty of money for shoes.
With a disgusted swipe of her hand, Keely swept a
half-dozen shoe boxes into her arms. They wobbled in
her grasp and one extremely heavy one tumbled free,
spilling a thick white envelope onto the carpet.

Dumping the rest of the shoe boxes onto the bed,
Keely knelt down and picked up the envelope. Think-

ing it might contain bills or tax receipts, she tore open the flap. She felt the blood drain from her face, and her fingertips trembled with a curious, uncertain fear. Something was wrong, terribly wrong, she thought as she sank to the floor.

The envelope contained a voucher from a well-known cruise line for a week-long cruise to Mexico. All the documents were in the name of Mr. and Mrs. Bannister, Rosie and Todd.

But the receipt attached to the travel voucher was made out to Martin Sargent—the loan shark who'd died with her sister.

Biting her lip, Keely clutched the papers to her breast and thought of the implications of her discovery. Rosie and Todd never had any money; they couldn't afford a Mexican cruise. So where did these vouchers come from? What did they mean? Could the rumors started by the newspaper possibly be right? Oh, God, she hoped not. It would break Pop's heart.

What was she going to do? She couldn't put the tickets back in the closet and pretend she'd never found them. But if she turned them in to the authorities, they would be construed as evidence of Rosie's involvement in some illegal activity. If only poor Rosie were here to defend herself. And what about Todd? Was he also involved?

If only she could share this burden with her father. But more worry was the last thing he needed right now. Although Mike Travers never complained, Keely knew the chemotherapy he was undergoing and the shock of Rosie's death were taking a severe toll on his strength.

She had to talk this over with someone. Who could she trust to keep her secret? Although her father had taken a medical retirement from the San Diego Police Department over six months ago, Keely knew he kept in close contact with his former colleagues. It would be devastating if he heard about this from someone outside the family.

After pacing the length of the small bedroom for nearly ten minutes, Keely came to her decision. In order not to step on any toes, she'd better start at the top with her father's best friend, Police Chief Lyle Kapinski.

Taking a deep breath, Keely picked up the bedside phone and dialed the chief's home number.

"Hi, Chief? Keely Travers here."

"Keely! I told you never to phone me at home—my wife's getting suspicious." He chuckled loudly at his own joke. Martha Kapinski had been like a second mother to the Travers girls.

Forcing a cheery tone, Keely replied, "If I were you, I wouldn't do anything to provoke Martha, Chief. I've heard she swings a mean rolling pin."

He sighed deeply, imitating a long-suffering husband. "And I have the knots on my head to prove it. So, if you don't want to have an affair, what *can* I do for you?" His voice turned somber, as if he'd just remembered about Rosie. "How are you holding up, honey? How's Mike?"

"You know Dad, he never complains. I haven't talked with him yet today, but...actually, he's part of the reason I called you."

She heard the sharp intake of the chief's breath. "Mike hasn't taken a turn for the worse, has he?"

Now that she had the chief on the line, Keely was suddenly unsure about involving him. What had she been thinking of? Lyle Kapinski wasn't just an old family friend, he was also the chief of police. If she told him about her suspicious find in Rosie's closet, he'd be forced to launch an investigation. It would kill her father if something unsavory was uncovered about Rosie.

Stalling, Keely said, "Dad *seems* okay. I don't want to burden him with anything else. I just don't understand what was going on with my sister. Why was she involved with a creep like Marty Sargent?"

He hesitated for a long tense moment, then released a deep, rumbling sigh. "I was going to talk to your father tomorrow, but maybe you're right. I won't lie to you, honey, things sure don't look good right now. Matter of fact, I've been on the phone most of the afternoon with a G-man in Washington. Seems our boy Sargent is connected to a syndicate back East."

He paused, and said hesitantly, "The agent heading up the investigation is flying out tonight."

Twirling the phone cord around her fingertip, Keely stared into space. Now, more than ever, she felt she should keep the cruise tickets to herself. An outside government agent wouldn't know her sister and would certainly misconstrue the meager "evidence" against her.

No, she decided, no good could come of tarnishing her sister's reputation beyond repair. "I...I just can't believe Rosie would do something illegal."

"Let's hope you're right, Keely. Tell you what. Let me make a few more phone calls. Let's find out all we can on this Sargent character before we go any farther. See what his game was."

"How long do you think it'll take?"

"I'll have something by morning, if I have to put the whole department on overtime. Don't do anything or say a word to anyone until I talk with you. Got it?"

"All right, Chief. Guess I'll talk to you tomorrow. I sure appreciate your help."

His voice softened. Gone was the hard-nosed police chief, replaced by the kindly man who'd dandled her on his knee when she was a small child. "Try not to worry, honey. We'll get to the bottom of this, I promise. When we do, I just know we're going to clear Rosie's name."

Keely felt hot tears forming behind her eyes. She truly hoped he was right.

THE NEXT MORNING, as she crossed the threshold into the squad room, Keely felt tension settle over the room like a damp fog. The room was so quiet she could hear every jagged breath, every surreptitious rattle of paper as her co-workers bent over their desks, focusing on anything except her.

Obviously the rumor of Rosie's alleged unlawful activities had already filtered through the department to Keely's colleagues. They were embarrassed for her and, God help her, she was embarrassed for herself. She closed her eyes in a silent prayer that the chief would find something, some fragment of evidence, that would prove Rosie's involvement with the loan shark had been personal, not criminal.

Keely tossed her purse in her desk drawer and leaned over, sorting through the heaps of papers and file folders on her desk.

Her partner, Bob Craybill, was on the phone, murmuring quietly.

She waited until he finished the call and said, "Hey, Bob. What's up?"

"What the hell are you doing here?"

She shrugged and riffled through a stack of pink message slips. Nothing pressing. Mostly expressions of condolence.

He leaned back in his chair and watched her. Eighteen years on the job had cost him most of his hair and added a heavy network of lines to his face. "You know, this department could probably function if you stayed home with your dad another day or two."

Keely shook her head forcefully. "No. I need to work."

He nodded. "No sense arguing with you, partner. You're as stubborn as your old man. By the way, Chief Kapinski himself phoned about ten minutes ago. Said as soon as you got in to come to his office."

Keely looked longingly at the coffeemaker as it sputtered out the last of a freshly brewed pot into the carafe. "Guess I'd better head on over there."

"Guess so. What's up?" Bob asked, his curiosity showing on his plain features. "He said ASAP twice."

"Hmm. Probably about Rosie's memorial." She hated the lie but she had given her word to the chief.

"Anything I can do to help? Make calls, anything?"

"No, but thanks." Normally as crusty as a hard roll, Bob had a soft mushy side that few ever saw. Keely suddenly felt grateful he was her partner. A cop could do a lot worse. His only shortcoming was a propensity for indulging in watercooler gossip. All the more reason to keep the discovery she'd made at Rosie's to herself.

"Well, even if you just need a skinny shoulder to cry on, I'm here."

Still yearning for that fresh cup of coffee, she yanked her purse out of the drawer and hurried upstairs. Chief Kapinski had a well-deserved reputation for being a thorough, if plodding, manager. But he'd said ASAP twice. That was real excitement, coming from the laid-back police chief.

Rounding the corner of "executive row," Keely nodded a greeting to the chief's secretary, Erma Rodriguez. As usual, Erma had the phone tucked against her ear and merely waved as Keely passed.

The chief's door was partially open so she tapped lightly and stepped inside. "I hope you had some luck, Chief, because—"

She broke off abruptly. A man was standing with his back to the room, staring out the window to the harbor below. There was something disturbingly familiar about the way he tilted his head, something that caused her blood to move restively in her veins.

While she had been expecting to see the chief's stocky figure in his rumpled department-store suit, this man...this man was tall and lean. Even from the rear, she could see how the expensive cut of his charcoal suit enhanced his broad, powerful shoulders. His carefully styled hair was the rich color of pecan shells and feathered the top of his collar. This man was sleek and elegant. Powerful. Alarming.

Then the stranger turned slowly and pinned Keely with his blue-gray eyes.

Her heart stopped. It couldn't be. But after returning his unblinking stare for a long moment, she accepted the truth. Noah Bannister had returned to San Diego.

"Hi, Keely," he said at last, taking several loping strides toward her. When only a couple of feet away, he focused those searing eyes at her and extended his hand. "I was really sorry to hear about Rosie. If there's anything I can do, anything at all, please don't hesitate to—"

Without thinking, Keely reached out and slapped him smartly across the face.

Chapter Two

"Ah, I see you two have already renewed your acquaintance." Chief Kapinski's voice boomed behind her. He walked past them without wasting a curious glance on the tableau. "Now if you're through reminiscing over old times, maybe we can get down to business."

Keely's hand hung in midair, still stinging from the blow she'd given Noah. She looked in horror at her bright red palm. Never in her entire life had Keely struck another person. She couldn't bring herself to look up and face Noah. Not that he didn't deserve it.

"Keely? If you've finished mauling our agent, maybe you'd like to sit down."

Lyle Kapinski had settled his bulk into his worn leather chair and was gesturing to the empty pair of visitor seats in front of his desk.

Noah Bannister must have been the "G-man" the chief had referred to on the phone last night. Why hadn't he told her? The answer came immediately: if she'd known who was waiting for her this morning, she'd have never walked through that door.

Keeping her eyes carefully averted, she dropped her purse on the chief's desk and eased into the chair farthest from Noah's looming presence. He hadn't spoken a word since her attack. She couldn't believe he was actually here, calmly standing beside her. Now that the initial shock had dissipated, she had a sudden, incomprehensible urge to jump out of the chair, throw her arms around his waist and burrow her head against his chest. But, of course, she couldn't.

Noah Bannister had walked away from her without a backward glance. The heartache and humiliation she'd suffered afterward hadn't paled in the ten years since his departure. No, she couldn't—wouldn't—forgive him. Ever. He'd hurt her too badly.

A second later she sensed that he'd sat down beside her. Deliberately turning her head until Noah was out of her line of sight, she leaned toward the chief. "So what did you find out?"

He flipped open a manila folder and scanned the contents. "This Marty Sargent had a rap sheet, all right, but most of the charges were relatively minor. Assault and battery, usury, a couple conspiracies to commit bodily harm."

She nodded. She would have been surprised if he hadn't had a police record. The newspapers had even hinted at mob connections. She waited for Kapinski to continue, knowing there was a twist in this story—a twist that somehow involved Noah Bannister.

The chief leaned back in his chair and steepled his pudgy fingertips over his paunch. "When we picked up Sargent's personal effects from the coroner we found evidence of a connection to Mexico."

Keely's heart thumped. Mexico? Did this have something to do with those cruise tickets hidden in Rosie's closet?

"Of course," Kapinski continued, "our first guess was that Sargent was involved in drug trafficking and planned on using Rosie as a mule. The odd thing was that he didn't have any kind of drug charges on his rap sheet. According to Vice, there wasn't any rumble on the street that Sargent was planning on expanding from small-time loan sharking into drug dealing." He broke off and pulled a handful of hard candies from his pocket.

Since the chief had quit smoking last year, his stash of hard candies was as much a part of him as his ever-expanding middle.

Keely rubbed her eyes; she was so weary, so bewildered. Gambling, cruise tickets and now illicit drugs. What did any of this have to do with her sister—or Noah, for that matter?

She stole a glance at him. He was slumped down, elbow resting on the chair arm, his chin propped up by his thumb and forefinger. He looked as relaxed as the devil in his own den.

Kapinski popped a sour ball into his mouth. "Anyway, when we uncovered the possible drug connection, I got on the horn to a buddy of mine in the DEA. Sargent was clean insofar as the DEA was concerned, but he'd heard a rumor that the Treasury Department had an interest in our boy."

Noah stirred in his chair and fastened his wintry gaze on Keely for a moment. Big mistake. Even though he had already planned to return to San Diego for Rosie's memorial service, he shouldn't have agreed to handle this lead. California still had too many ghosts, too many reminders of a painful past. But this was his case, his baby. It would have taken days to bring another agent up to speed.

Who was he kidding? Even if he hadn't already been on-site, Noah knew that the moment Kapinski's report came in, he would've started packing. Even if Rosie hadn't been involved, Noah would have jumped at the opportunity to come back to San Diego—to see Keely again.

Apparently she wasn't as thrilled to see him. His jaw was still stinging from the well-deserved smack across the chops she'd landed. Keely the girl had worshiped the very ground he walked on. Obviously Keely the woman had a slightly different opinion of his charms.

While Kapinski continued to fill her in on Sargent's background, Noah let his mind drift backward. He'd been no more than a boy when he'd decided to get the hell out of San Diego, away from Keely's mistrust. Sure, he could have taken her into his confidence; but he shouldn't have had to make that choice. If she had loved him as much as she claimed, Keely wouldn't have believed the lies. She would have trusted him.

Back then, though, not many people had been on his side. He couldn't blame them, not really. It was easier to label him as another wayward kid from a broken home who'd run afoul of the law. He'd counted on Keely's loyalty.

He'd been bitterly disappointed.

The chief was winding down his summation and raised a hand toward Noah. "Since Bannister here was coming in from D.C. anyway, the Treasury Department put him on loan to us to lend his expertise. Your show, Bannister."

Noah tossed Keely another glance. She was still staring straight ahead, her eyes focused intently on the chief's dusty college diploma on the wall behind him.

Noah twisted in his chair until he could comfortably
address them both. Keely's reaction to his upcoming
suggestion could make or break this case.

Clearing his throat, he launched into a background
sketch of Martin Sargent. "Your dead perp first came
to our attention a few months ago when he was operating a minor-league loan-sharking operation in Atlantic City. One of our guys was on a routine stakeout,
gathering evidence on a gang of enterprising counterfeiters, when he saw him come out of a restaurant with
one of the really big bosses.

"Almost overnight, Sargent started dressing real
uptown. Began sporting a shiny new car. It was obvious he'd climbed into bed with some high-powered
wise guys.

"A short time later Sargent abruptly moved out
here to the Coast and set up a completely new operation. We know he was still connected to the Atlantic
City group because he was flying to Jersey every week
or two."

Her gaze still fixed on the wall behind the police
chief, Keely said tightly, "I don't get it. What would
a two-bit loan shark have to do with a large counterfeiting organization?"

Noah shrugged. "At this point our best guess is that
he's not much more than a delivery boy. Several of the
more, shall we say, sought after, engravers have moved
their operations to Mexico and South America. San
Diego is a natural conduit across the border back into
the U.S. In fact, we've got strong reason to believe that
the actual printing and distribution of the phony bills
is done here, as well."

"What!" Chief Kapinski's chin jutted forward. "I
think you've got some bad information, Bannister.

There's no way anything like that could be going down in my town without someone in my department hearing a rumor. No way.''

Noah exhaled deeply and rolled his head on his shoulders, releasing tension. He hadn't wanted to get into this part right now, but Kapinski was shrewd. Maybe too shrewd. Keeping a watchful eye on the chief's expression, he plunged ahead. ''The fact that your department is completely in the dark about this is a matter of some concern to the Treasury Department, Chief. The most logical inference is that someone in your department is on the take.''

Kapinski heaved his bulk out of his chair with amazing speed. ''Now see here, Bannister! I run a clean outfit. We have some of the most outstanding police officers in the nation and I won't have their reputations impugned by a—''

''Chief, Chief!'' Noah held up his hands, halting the flow of indignation. ''Believe me, I'm not maligning you or your department. But no matter how good the organization, no matter how honorable most of the officers are, you and I both know that a small percentage of police officers are going to be vulnerable to bribery. That's a fact of life.''

''That may be a fact of life in your department, Bannister, but believe me, it isn't around here. It's always been my policy to offer the feds complete cooperation, but not at the expense of my staff's reputation.''

Kapinski nodded once, as if to emphasize his point, and eased back into his chair. He slowly unwrapped a cinnamon candy and slipped it between his pursed lips. ''We'll have no more talk about cops on the take and departmental leaks. Understand, Bannister?''

Noah stared at the police chief for a long tense moment before he bobbed his head. He decided to humor Kapinski—at least for the time being. "In all fairness, Chief, we're not sure where the leak is originating. Hell, it could be someone in the Treasury Department. But the truth is, every time we come close to nailing that syndicate, they slide out of the trap."

Leaning back in his chair, fingers laced across his belly, the chief apparently had his temper back under control. "So what do you think is going down now? What was the connection between Sargent and Rosie?"

"My hunch is that our Atlantic City boys are expecting some new engraving plates and enlisted Marty Sargent to safeguard their delivery. I don't know how, but I think Sargent was going to use Rosie to help transport those plates. Of course, I don't have a shred of evidence to support that hunch."

Keely's temper engulfed the tiny spark of conscience that reminded her she had the evidence Noah needed. She was furious at his willingness to throw dirt at her dead sister's reputation without proof. "You're really making points, Noah. First you malign the reputation of every cop on this force, now you start on my sister, who isn't . . . isn't here to defend herself!"

Noah closed his eyes and sighed deeply. Then he turned and pierced Keely with his cold, unblinking stare. "I didn't come here to try to make points. I came to nail a crime syndicate that's spreading millions of dollars of phony money up and down the East Coast."

"But my sister—"

"Let me finish, please." He raised his hand to stem the tide of her rebuttal. "I'm sorry Rosie was killed, I truly am. You know as much as anybody that I always had a soft spot for her, but I can't let that interfere with my professional judgment. We all know that Rosie's had a, shall we say, troubled past. First was her teenage foray into recreational drugs. Your father spent a fortune on rehab programs, then she turned to booze. And gambling.''

Keely could hold her silence no longer. "She changed! She'd made a lot of progress these past few months.''

Noah's disbelief was obvious. "Oh, really? Did you know that until a month ago, she continued to bounce checks with great regularity? Checks that she cashed at the casinos on the various reservations around the county.''

"That doesn't mean she'd agree to smuggle for a crime syndicate,'' Keely insisted stubbornly.

"How much proof do you need? Not only was she with the creep when his Mercedes ran off the road, they had a history. She stopped bouncing checks about the same time that Marty Sargent arranged a line of credit for her at the local casino. You didn't know that, either?'' he asked archly.

Numb and sick with this new and convincing evidence, Keely mutely shook her head.

In a somewhat gentler tone, Noah said sadly, "I know you did your best for her. So did Todd. But you can't help someone until they're ready to be helped.''

At the mention of Noah's brother, Keely looked up. Todd must have known what was going on; his name was on those cruise tickets along with Rosie's. "Aren't you forgetting something? My sister was a married woman, happily married, I might add. So if she was involved in *anything,* it only makes sense that Todd knew about it, as well.''

A haunted look shadowed Noah's face for a brief instant. "You're right, of course. I can't ignore the possibility that my brother is involved. Although I hope we can prove that both of them were innocent.''

Both of them or just Todd? Until Todd's name came up, Noah hadn't spoken as if clearing Rosie's reputation was very high on his priority list. In Keely's opinion, Noah's theory had more holes in it than a slice of Swiss cheese.

Keely locked her gaze with Noah's. "It seems to me that you're supposing an awful lot with very few facts. The only thing we know for sure is that my sister and Marty Sargent were in the same car when it plunged off that cliff. Maybe their being together was perfectly innocent. Maybe she didn't know what he did for a living.''

Never breaking eye contact, Noah said quietly, "I'm sorry, Keely, that's just not true. We've gone through Sargent's papers. Your sister owed him money—a lot of money.''

She blinked rapidly to quell the sudden onrush of tears. If Rosie owed a lot of money, there was no innocent explanation for an extravagant Mexican vacation. Keely felt her faith in her sibling's honesty eroding with each passing moment.

A dark scowl on his face, the chief leaned across his desk. "Something's bothering me, Bannister. If Sargent was getting paid to transport these plates, wouldn't it be kind of foolish for him to involve a civilian?''

Noah shook his head. "Actually, that would be a surprisingly clever move on Sargent's part. He might have had a tip that we were watching him. Innocent civilians are often duped into acting as mules—smugglers for high-risk drug deals. He could cover his own butt by using a tried-and-true method to move counterfeit plates.''

For the first time Keely swiveled her head to look at him. Noah felt his breath leap. Even after all these years, she had the power to set his blood racing with a mere glance.

Her lovely face, now more refined and elegant with the bloom of maturity, was screwed into a confused frown. ''Isn't that risky? I mean, wouldn't Sargent have expected Rosie to go to the authorities? After all, I just made detective and Dad's a retired captain. Heck, almost everyone we know is in law enforcement in some capacity.''

''I don't think Sargent could be expected to know that,'' Noah replied. ''It's highly doubtful Rosie was up front about her connections with the SDPD. According to Todd, she'd been playing poker at the reservation quite a bit lately. I'd be willing to bet that's where she met Sargent and later borrowed from him to cover her losses.''

Keely wouldn't take that bet. Now that Noah mentioned it, though, she'd noticed Rosie's distraction lately. In fact, just last month Rosie had borrowed from Keely to make her house payment. Still, she wouldn't admit defeat so easily; Rosie was no criminal and no one could convince her otherwise. ''So even if she *was* losing money at the casino, how does that tie her to Sargent?''

Noah snorted. ''You'll forgive my bluntness, but the mere fact that she was found with Sargent out in the boondocks tells us they were involved. Sargent probably watched her for a few weeks as she dug herself a deeper and deeper hole. He probably engaged her in superficial conversation, found out she was a lifetime resident, employed, married. Except for her gambling, he saw her as basically stable. Exactly the kind of carrier he'd be looking for. Then, when she lost so much she became desperate, Sargent made his move.''

Keely closed her eyes and asked quietly, ''So you believe that Rosie was involved in smuggling?''

Seeing the pain reflected in Keely's dark, expressive eyes, Noah couldn't bring himself to admit what he suspected was the truth. He only hoped his brother hadn't been stupid enough to go along with the scheme.

Noah stared at the stricken look on Keely's face and was surprised by the thudding ache in the middle of his chest. Damn the woman! Even after all this time she had the power to make him feel like a louse for hurting her. He tried to think of something he could say, some words of comfort—if only to ease his own conscience. Although he didn't believe it for a moment, he was startled to hear himself mutter, ''There's still a chance Rosie was an innocent dupe.''

Kapinski leaned forward and pounded a meaty fist on the desk. ''Well, I'm only sorry I can't arrest that lowlife for extortion and usury!''

Keely shook her head. ''None of this helps clear my sister's name. But something else has been bothering me. Do you think there's a chance that that crash wasn't accidental? I mean, what if Sargent's mob bosses found out he'd subcontracted the delivery?''

Noah stretched out his legs, his long slender fingers plucking at the perfect seam in his slacks. ''Excellent point, Keely. Right now we don't have any evidence that their deaths weren't accidental.''

Pushing out of her chair, Keely stormed over to the window. "So that's it?" she asked over her shoulder. "My sister's dead and her reputation is in shreds but the counterfeiters just keep on with business as usual?"

Noah stood and crossed the room to stand behind Keely. The soft powdery scent of her perfume tickled his nostrils, reminding him of the sweetness of the kisses they'd once shared. Unable to think clearly with her so near, he backed away. "There is one possible alternative. What if their deaths *were* accidental? Suppose word of Sargent's death hasn't reached his mob bosses yet? What if they haven't canceled the transfer of those plates?"

Keely whirled around. "You think that transfer is going to take place in Mexico, don't you?"

Noah and the chief exchanged a glance. The chief nodded slightly and Noah picked up a gray folder from the desk. "Remember that piece of evidence the chief mentioned that tied Sargent to Mexico? We found this in his wallet." He opened the folder and extracted a slip of notepaper encased in a plastic evidence sleeve.

With a trembling hand, Keely took the paper. Written with a broad-tipped marker, the message was clear: *Viva Zapata's Cantina, noon Tuesday, Aug. 22. Roberto.*

She read it twice and returned it to the gray folder. Viva Zapata's was a well-known tourist trap in Ensenada, Mexico, a stop for every cruise ship going south of the border. Keely could no longer deny her sister's involvement. But if she told them about the cruise tickets—

"Keely?" Noah's voice sounded faraway, fuzzy but concerned. "What's wrong?"

Ignoring the fiery lump in her throat, she whispered, "That's next Tuesday. You think that's when the transfer is going to be made, don't you?"

Noah frowned. "It's the only thing that makes sense. And if we're lucky, I think we can intercept that package."

Keely picked up his line of thought. "And by following those plates like crumbs in Hansel and Gretel's forest, you think—"

"We have a chance to nail everyone who touches that package, including whoever is using his badge to protect the counterfeit operation." What Noah didn't mention was his suspicion that the girls' father, Mike Travers, was the leak. As watch commander, he had been privy to every bit of gossip and information that made its way through the department. Such a hunch also went a long way toward explaining why Rosie Travers Bannister would have allowed herself to be used: she was trying to protect her father.

Keely slowly twisted her neck and stared out the window into the bright morning sun. What was she going to do? If she continued to keep those cruise tickets to herself, she would be interfering with a police investigation—breaking the law. She'd taken an oath to uphold the law. But if she gave them the evidence she'd uncovered, she knew Rosie would be condemned. It would break their father's heart.

Despite the quickly mounting pile of evidence to the contrary, Keely still believed in her sister's innocence. Somehow it was up to her to prove it. She had to tell them about the tickets; her own innate honesty and the oath she'd taken when she joined the force demanded it.

With an audible sigh, she crossed the room and picked up her purse from the chief's desk. Her fingers shook and her stomach roiled with trepidation as she pulled out the cruise tickets.

She handed the envelope to Noah and walked quickly back to the window. Turning her head, she murmured against the glass, "I found these in Rosie's closet last night."

He examined the documents for a few seconds and flipped the envelope to the police chief. He turned to Keely, admiration evident in his blue-gray eyes. "You realize the contact is going to be on that cruise, don't you?"

Keely shrugged. "So what happens now?"

He leaned forward and retrieved the envelope from the corner of the chief's desk. Keeping his gaze tightly on her reaction, Noah slapped the envelope against the palm of his hand. "I suggest we use these tickets. See where they take us."

"Us? Do you mean you and I?" Her hand flew to her throat and fluttered like a small, trapped dove against her collar.

"Exactly. Who's better qualified to impersonate my brother and your sister?"

"But, but—"

"You are a police officer, aren't you?"

"Sure. But I've never done any kind of undercover work. Shouldn't you use someone with more experience?"

Closing his mind to the tangible sexual aura that surrounded her, Noah stood and moved quietly to her

side. He hated using Keely this way, but he'd been
after the head of this organization for a long time and
this was the closest he'd come to getting a break in the
case. Dangling the envelope from his fingertips like a
lure, he pressed, "Maybe, but I don't think anyone
else could impersonate Rosie. You're her sister, you
know her like a book you read last night. There's
bound to be some kind of test. They aren't going to
hand over a set of currency plates worth millions simply because someone says she's Rosemary Bannister.
You're the one person who would know enough to
validate Rosie's identity. Besides, if your hair was a
little shorter, you'd look enough like Rosie to pass for
her. Your voices are similar enough to fool anyone."

Sensing a weakening in her resolve, he pressed his
last point, the one that made him feel like a jerk for
even mentioning it. "You do want to clear your sister's name, don't you?"

She nodded.

Noah handed her the envelope, knowing he'd won.
"These reservations are for the day after tomorrow.
We don't have much time to put a plan together. It's
your call, Keely."

Keely stared down at the envelope as if it was alive
and writhing. She couldn't do this, just couldn't. He
didn't realize what he was asking. If she agreed to this
impersonation, she was agreeing to pose as Noah
Bannister's wife. To travel with him, share a tiny
stateroom with him, pretend to cuddle like newlyweds while they were in public.

A white heat filled her as she considered the implications. Dear Lord, she couldn't do this thing. She'd
do anything to help clear Rosie's reputation, but not
this. Not audition for a role she'd never have.

"All right," she heard herself say. "Tell me what to do."

"Good." Noah's relief was palpable. "Don't worry, I'll be at your side every moment. Nothing will happen to you, I promise. Believe me, this is the only solution. You won't be sorry."

"I already am," she stated flatly. "So let's get started before I change my mind."

AFTER TWO HOURS of hashing out a rudimentary plan, Keely left the chief's office. While Noah and the chief ironed out the details, Keely took advantage of their inattention to make her escape. Noah's nearness as he leaned over her shoulder had suddenly become stifling. Suffocating. Intimidating. Until she felt she would scream if she didn't get away.

When she tried to slip out of the anteroom, Erma Rodriguez hastily hung up the telephone. "Keely! Come here a minute."

"How's it going, Erma?"

The short woman waved a pudgy hand. "I got five kids—all teenagers—at home. How do you think it's going?" Erma pointed to her boss's office. "How are you doin', hon? I'm so sorry about your sister."

Keely shrugged. She didn't know how to respond when her friends offered their condolences. Maybe she was still in shock, too unnerved by Rosie's sudden death to fully feel the depth of her loss.

As if sensing Keely's discomfort, Erma patted the younger woman's hand and made a valiant, if obvious, effort to change the subject. "So, what was going on in there, anyway? Who's that hunk? Nobody tells me nothing!"

Despite her gloomy mood, Keely grinned. "Give me a break, Erma. You know everything that goes on around here."

"I wish! Seriously, Keely, what were you guys doing in there so long? The boss said he'd have me arrested if I let anyone interrupt. So who's the guy in the sharp suit? *¿Mucho macho, sí?*"

Keely's lip curled in a grimace. That Noah Bannister was an attractive man was beyond dispute. Unfortunately, he'd long ago proven himself to be a good-looking jerk.

At that moment the handsome jerk appeared in the doorway behind her. "Got a minute?"

"If it's necessary," she answered coldly.

He fell into step beside her as they walked to the elevator. "We may not have much of a chance to talk privately tomorrow so I thought we should iron out the details now. If you don't have any objections, I'll pick you up at your place about noon on Friday."

"I can meet you at the pier."

He shook his head. "Wouldn't it look a little strange for the newlyweds to show up separately?"

Noah held the open elevator door until she was safely inside. Pushing the lobby button, he continued in a conversational tone, "Any chance we can have dinner together tonight? To kind of...talk things over?"

Talk? *Now* he wanted to talk? "I think you're about ten years too late!" she snapped.

She walked away, her heels clicking on the polished marble floor in a staccato echo of her rage.

She'd only gone a few feet when Lieutenant Dale Cabot appeared out of nowhere and grabbed her arm. "Whoa! Slow down, girl. Where's the fire?"

Stopping, she blew out a deep breath and looked up into his incredible blue eyes. Most of the women Keely knew would kill for a date with Dale Cabot, so what was wrong with her?

Why was she so immune to his obvious appeal? And why, oh why, did she still feel that quiver in her stomach when Noah Bannister walked in the door?

Taking her by the elbow, Cabot led her into the deserted room where they held roll call at the beginning of each shift. He kicked the door closed behind them and backed Keely against the wall. Staring into her eyes with his own startling blue gaze, he asked, "So where have you been hiding? I phoned you several times since I got the word about your sister."

She forced a smile and tried to slip from his grasp. When he refused to release her she said mildly, "I had the phone off the hook."

"Why? To avoid me?"

"Cab, that's not true! I had a lot going on, that's all. You know my dad's been sick and Todd fell apart, so I had to make all the arrangements and—"

"Quit making excuses. You've been avoiding me for days, Keely. Since long before the accident. Why? Because you knew Bannister was coming back to town and you were holding out for your old love?"

Shoving against his arms in earnest now, she wriggled from his grasp. "This isn't like you, Cab—"

"How would you know? You don't know a damned thing about me, and you never wanted to learn. Why won't you at least talk to me? Hear me out."

"Because we've been through this before."

"I know, I know, you're not ready for a relationship. Isn't that supposed to be the guy's line?"

Keely felt the heavy pressure of a migraine building up behind her eyes. "Cab, please. This really isn't the time."

"No, you're right. I'm acting like a jerk and I'm sorry. It's just that I don't understand you, Keely. You refuse to even give our relationship a chance. Why? Because you're still mooning over some guy who threw you over when you were in high school. Wake up before it's too late! Trust me—when *I* walk out, I won't be back. You'll be tossing away the best thing that ever happened to you."

"I know, Cab. Believe me, I know. And it isn't Noah Bannister. Not really. It's me. I've tried to tell you without hurting you, but... but I just don't have the right kind of feelings for you. Why can't we just stay friends?"

"Friends?" Dropping his hands to his sides, he regarded her with his cold stare for several long seconds. "All right, Keely. You've made your bed—now go see if you can lure Bannister into it. Remember one thing—when you wake up the next morning, don't be surprised to find out he's gone."

He slammed out the door and left her swimming in the wake of his wounded pride. She was sorry it had ended on such a sour note, but not sorry that it was over. Cab had said he didn't understand her. Sometimes Keely didn't understand herself. The unvarnished truth was that she was holding out for bells and whistles, a man who made her toes curl when he kissed her.

The pounding behind her eyes was beating like a furious drumbeat now. Keely knew it was her own guilty conscience that was responsible. She shouldn't have gone out with Dale Cabot in the first place. Cab was a nice guy; he deserved more than she was able to give him, more than she might be able to give any man. Things like intimacy, trust, unconditional love. Noah had spoiled all that for her.

Raking her fingers through her ebony hair, she thought of the mountain of tasks she still had to do. She would have to rearrange her duty schedule to cover her absence, get some money and her passport from the bank, have her hair cut and pack her clothes.

And somehow find the strength to attend her sister's funeral.

Stopping by personnel, Keely filled out the paperwork for a vacation, commencing immediately, to assuage any curiosity within the department. The chief had assured her that he would personally see to it that the leave chit disappeared before it reached payroll. She was to receive her full pay while on this assignment.

Another tense moment had occurred in the chief's office when he'd started to write a voucher for expenses. Noah had stopped him, saying the tab for all expenses would be picked up by the Treasury Department. She could submit a request for reimbursement after they returned from the cruise.

The implication was that any paperwork handled through the local police was subject to departmental gossip. Although Noah left the words unspoken, they shimmered in the air and the chief once again fired off an outraged denial.

Noah was able to soothe Kapinski's indignation, but the atmosphere was charged with hostility. That was when Keely made her hasty exit, leaving the two men to work out their dispute.

Back at her own desk, Keely ignored Bob Craybill's curious gaze while she reassigned the work pending on her agenda. When she finally looked up again, he was gone. Oh well, at least by leaving him a memo she wouldn't have to fabricate any more lies to quench his curiosity.

Chapter Three

Keely stared blankly at the slip of paper the teller had pushed across the counter. "There must be some mistake," she said. "This can't possibly be my balance."

According to the sum penciled on the scrap of paper, Keely's balance was higher than it should have been. About ten thousand dollars higher.

"The bank doesn't make mistakes, Ms. Travers," the stout woman replied with forced politeness. "I assure you that is your proper balance. Of course, any recent deposits or checks not yet cashed would affect that sum. Will there be anything else?"

Keely groaned inwardly and started to walk away. She didn't need this, she really didn't. Especially not today, with her sister's funeral only two hours away. Still, she was leaving early in the morning with Noah on their "honeymoon," and she didn't want to leave this error pending until her return next week.

Wheeling around, she prepared for battle with the iron-willed bank teller. "As a matter of fact, there is something else you can help me with. I'd like a print-out of all my checking-account transactions for the past month."

The teller pursed her lips and stared at her recalcitrant customer. "There will be a two-dollar charge for that printout, Ms. Travers."

"Fine." Keely laughed wryly. "Take it out of this extra ten thousand dollars."

The woman moved a few feet away to a centralized desk and clicked away at a keyboard. While Keely waited for the computer to complete its task, her nerves began to quiver, then reverberate as a feeling of dread washed over her. If this wasn't a mistake, where did that money come from? Rosie? But how and why?

A moment later a printer spat out a sheet of paper. The teller tore off the perforated sheet and studied it for a few seconds. Then she took a red felt-tip pen and circled one entry.

Her voice triumphant, she handed the printout to Keely. "As I told you, Ms. Travers, Penwick Trust and Savings doesn't make mistakes. Perhaps you forgot about this large deposit made last week."

Keely stared, disbelieving, at the circled entry. According to the bank records, ten thousand dollars was deposited into her account last Monday. "Would you have a copy of the check that was deposited?" she asked, still hopeful of discovering an error had been made. Perhaps someone had punched in the wrong account number.

The teller shook her head and tapped the computer-generated page with a manicured nail. "See this code? That means it was a cash transaction."

"But I don't have that kind of money! There must be some way to find out who put it in my account."

"Well, I suppose you could speak with Mr. Franklin, the branch manager. Our security cameras are time-coded. It's possible the security service we use could match the time of the deposit with the appropriate videotape and perhaps identify the person who made the deposit.''

''Oh, that's wonderful!'' Keely breathed deeply in relief. That tape would surely prove an error had been made. ''Where would I find Mr. Franklin?''

The woman pointed to an empty desk behind a glass partition. ''That's his office but he's on vacation until next Wednesday.''

''Then who is the assistant manager? Somebody must be in charge around here.'' Keely felt her frustration level rising with each passing second and forced herself to draw a deep, calming breath.

''Mrs. Wheeler is the assistant manager. She's out to lunch but will be back around two.''

Keely looked at her watch with impatience. ''That's too late. I need to know right now. Surely someone else can help me.''

The teller shook her head emphatically. ''No, I'm sorry, Ms. Travers. I could help you fill out the request form, but it would still have to be approved by either Mr. Franklin or Mrs. Wheeler. Besides, those tapes are stored off-site by our security consultants. It would take several days to locate the right tape and retrieve it from storage. Shall I have Mrs. Wheeler contact you later this afternoon?''

''No,'' Keely replied slowly, withdrawing her gold shield from her purse. ''I really need some information right now,'' she said as she flipped open the thick wallet. ''This is police business and I'd appreciate your cooperation.''

The teller inspected the badge carefully before returning it. ''I'm sorry, Ms. Travers, but there's simply nothing I can do. Even if you had a search warrant, I'd still have to refer you to our security department. As I said, the tapes are in their custody."

Keely dug her notepad and pen out of her pocket. "Who handles your security?"

The teller reached beneath the counter and pulled out a dog-eared business card. "Safeguard Security Systems. In Carlsbad."

Keely scribbled down the address and phone number with a sinking feeling. Carlsbad was forty miles away and she didn't have time to drive out there and back. Rosie's funeral service was scheduled for two. She barely had time to change clothes and get out to her father's house.

And first thing in the morning she was leaving for Mexico with Noah. "I'm going out of town myself. I'll be in touch when I return."

"Have a nice day then," the teller chirped brightly. "Next!"

Keely trudged out of the bank, her heart heavy with this new development. She didn't want to believe it, but she was terribly afraid that extra money had been placed in her account by her sister. There was no other answer. Who else would have had access to her deposit slips or account number? Rosie must have gotten the cash from Sargent and put it in Keely's account to keep Todd from finding out about it.

Even that made no sense. Had her sister honestly believed Keely wouldn't notice when her bank balance rose by ten thousand dollars? Even the naive Rosie hadn't been that much of an airhead. The only logical explanation was that she was going to tell Keely about the money but had been killed before she had the chance.

The question now was what was Keely going to do about that little "bonus" in her account? With Rosie implicated in Sargent's counterfeiting scheme, Keely knew if this huge deposit was discovered, her own honesty would be questioned. And right now she had no way to prove her own innocence.

No, she thought, stuffing the telltale printout into her handbag, she wasn't going to mention this money to a soul until she saw that videotape. This "bonus" had to be her own little secret for the next few days.

Still, as she walked to her car the money weighed on her conscience like a storm cloud, dark and ominous.

SITTING IN HIS mother's living room and staring out the picture window, Noah felt like a caged tiger. Sargent's death had provided the break he'd been waiting for. Noah had no doubts; there was going to be some kind of contact on that cruise ship and the actual transfer of the plates would take place in Mexico next Tuesday. He was finally going to bring down the counterfeiting ring.

Now that he had a solid lead, it was hard to sit idle. Of course, there was really nothing more he could do before boarding that cruise ship in Long Beach.

Except think.

Think was all he'd done for the past six months. He'd turned this puzzle over in his mind a thousand times and still came up with the same solution: One or more of the Travers family was involved in this mess.

But who?

He refused to accept the idea that Keely would take part in something illegal. Before Rosie's death, Noah had cared deeply about his sister-in-law. Her death was a horrible blow, and he'd miss her eccentric personality almost as much as Todd would. Still, as much as he hated to accept the truth, she was almost surely implicated.

Even worse, he was afraid she wasn't the only Travers involved. In fact, Noah considered the girls' father a prime suspect for the "leak" in the police department. Until his retirement a few months before, Mike Travers's path had crossed with Marty Sargent's on two separate official occasions. They'd discovered his signature on two of Sargent's arrest reports, neither of which had resulted in a conviction.

Based on that unusual circumstance, the Treasury Department had begun a stealthy yet thorough investigation into Travers's background. Only one irregularity had been found, but in Noah's opinion, it was a large one: Mike Travers's savings account had a very high balance for a career police officer. Noah couldn't help wondering where the money had come from.

And he was determined to find out—despite the sad likelihood that Keely was going to be hurt again.

A little red compact pulled into Mike Travers's driveway next door. Noah moved the sheer curtain aside with his fingertip and watched Keely alight from the car. She'd had her hair cut, a short cheeky style very similar to the way Rosie had worn her own hair. On Rosie it had been cute, saucy. But on Keely there was a subtle difference. She looked sleek, sophisticated. Darkly elegant.

Even in her somber black suit, there was an aura of sensuality about her.

She looked good. Too damned good.

AS KEELY PULLED INTO her father's driveway, she couldn't stop herself from glancing at the house next door. A plain silver car with rental plates was parked in Dorena Bannister's open garage.

Noah? Of course. Who else could it be?

A quick flush stole up Keely's cheeks at the knowledge of his nearness. At least it was good for Dorena that her prodigal son had finally come home—if only for a brief visit. The youthful widow rarely left home anymore, so swamped was she in her own private grief. Keely had often wondered whether it was the death of Dorena's husband or her son's desertion that had trampled her heart the most.

Noah had unceremoniously left those who cared about him when he'd fled San Diego, and all of them wondered why.

When she stepped out of the car, Keely saw her father pruning his tomato plants on the side of the house. Had she expected Mike Travers to take it easy as the doctor ordered? Not a chance, she thought wryly. Open rebellion seemed to be a family trait.

He tossed her a casual glance as she approached, then he pinched off an errant sucker vine with his shears.

Shielding her eyes against the blazing sun, she crunched along the gravel path until she stood behind her father. "What are you up to, Dad?"

He slowly turned in her direction and cocked a derisive eyebrow. "What does it look like I'm doing? Any fool could see I'm pruning my tomatoes."

Keely took no issue with her father's gruffness. Today was not easy for any of them. While she was thinking of the best approach to take, he tossed a withered vine aside and tucked his shears in his hip pocket.

Touching him lightly on the shoulder, she asked, "Don't you think you should be getting dressed? It's almost time."

Her father took off his hat and swiped his face with his forearm. "Yeah, I guess it is. Let's go inside. I made fresh tea."

She followed him out of the heat into the small kitchen that had changed little since her mother's death. Mike had added a dishwasher and replaced the dinette set when the old one fell apart; but essentially, this was still her mother's kitchen and Esther Travers's spirit permeated the atmosphere.

Mike seemed to regain his composure and patted his daughter's shoulder. He took off his cap, then bent over the sink and dashed his face and hands with crisp, cool water before pouring their ice tea.

When he'd seated himself across the table, Keely said, "Anything new?"

Mike pushed his glass aside and trailed his finger through the moist ring it left on the table. "Nope. Your sister's dead and I'm dying. Not a damned thing new."

Keely blinked. "How're you feeling, really, Pop?"

"Like the chemo might be worse than the cancer. But that's not why you came early, is it? You came to tell me Noah Bannister is back."

She gulped in astonishment. She'd always known the departmental grapevine was quick and sure, but, good grief, she'd only left the chief's office an hour ago. Then she recalled the silver rental car in Dorena's garage and realized her father must have seen Noah.

Taking several swallows of the icy beverage to give herself time to think, Keely finally said, "I, uh, guess he came back for the funeral."

"That's what I heard."

He finished his tea and set the empty glass back on the table with a loud, hollow thunk. "Keely, I've never been much for butting into your business, but I feel I'd be shirking my duty as your father if I didn't say something."

"Now, Dad—"

Mike held up a hand, forestalling her objections. "Didn't your folks teach you it was impolite to interrupt? Let me finish. All I want to say is that you've been nursing that wounded heart of yours too long. I know with Noah back in town it's only natural to dredge up the past. Maybe reopen those old wounds. Keely, honey, I'm telling you I think it's time you let go. Forgive the man."

Tears glimmering in her eyes, she bit her lower lip. "It's kind of hard to forgive someone who's never even acknowledged he did you any harm. Dammit, Noah owes me an explanation."

"Maybe he does, maybe not. Anyway, it's ancient history. The best thing you could do for yourself is be polite but keep your distance. I'd hate to see you hurt again, honey."

She nodded. No doubt her father was right, but it was going to be a considerable challenge to stay away from Noah when she was on a "honeymoon" with him.

Shifting uncomfortably in her chair, she chose her words carefully. "I always felt like...like you kind of took his side, Dad."

"Against you? Never. I could've strangled Noah Bannister for the way he took off and broke your heart."

"But you've always defended him."

Mike sighed deeply and drained his glass. "No. What I always tried to make you understand was that you were only seeing one side. I wanted you to consider there might have been things going on that Noah couldn't tell you about."

"What kind of things?" She frowned at her father's deliberately vague explanation.

"Oh, just . . . Hell, I don't know! I'm only saying you should let it go. It was a long time ago, honey. Things change. People change."

She leaned forward and clasped her father's thin, veiny hand. "I remember a certain crusty old cop telling me that a leopard isn't likely to turn into a zebra."

He shook his head sadly. "All I'm saying is that things aren't always what they seem."

She cast her father a curious glance, wondering how much he actually knew about Noah's departure all those years ago. Before Keely could question him further, however, he lifted his glass from the table and stood up. "I'm breaking a pledge by telling you this, but there was more to those adolescent pranks of Noah's than anybody knew. Remember, just because he was hauled into the station and suspended from high school a few times doesn't mean the boy was guilty. That's all I'm saying on the subject."

She pushed away from the table and paced the small confines until she got her temper back under control. "Dad, you're not being consistent here. If Noah wasn't guilty, why didn't you say something back then?"

Mike Travers shook his head decisively. "It was police business."

Police business? That didn't make any sense. Still, she knew she wouldn't get any information out of her stubborn parent. But she would have some answers. At her first opportunity, Keely intended to have a long-overdue discussion with Noah Bannister.

Catching her father's watchful eye, she murmured, "You're right, Dad. I have to go on with my life. I can't hate Noah forever."

But deep in her heart Keely knew she'd never really hated Noah. In fact, she sometimes wondered if she'd ever stopped loving him.

HOLDING ON TO her father's arm, uncertain whether for his support or her own, Keely made it through her sister's funeral. Bracketed by her grieving father and brother-in-law, she felt somehow detached. As if the scene wasn't real. Only a dreadful play, and soon the players would come on stage, bow and it would all be over.

But there was no curtain call. Suddenly, standing in the hot sun, she shivered, feeling as if she'd been immersed in a cold night fog. At the minister's intoned words meant to be comforting, Keely's eyes filled with tears as thick wet swirls of pain obscured her vision.

From a far off place, she saw her friends and co-workers gathered around the grave site. Through a roaring haze she heard her father murmur words of thanks to those who offered their condolences. Mostly, however, Keely was aware of the furtive glances being cast their way. Old friends who couldn't quite look her in the eye.

Everyone thought Rosie's death came as the result of criminal activities. Keely was going to prove them all wrong; she just had to.

Most especially, she had to prove Rosie's innocence to Noah Bannister, who stood silently at his brother's side, his granite-hard chin thrust outward as if inviting her challenge. Oh, she knew he harbored his own suspicions. As far as Keely was concerned, Noah was judging her sister using his own checkered past as a point of reference.

Finally the service ended and they were free to make their escape. After announcing that there would be a gathering at his home, Mike Travers wrapped his arm around his remaining daughter and they slowly walked to the waiting limousine.

By the time they changed cars at the funeral home and returned to Mike's small bungalow, the house was already teeming with people. Dorena Bannister, Noah and Todd's widowed mother, was acting as hostess, filling glasses and inviting everyone to partake in the bounty of food.

Seeing Keely and Mike enter, Dorena swiftly crossed the room. She scooted between them and hooked her arms into theirs, leading them to the dining room. "Come on, guys, let's get you something to eat."

The table was invisible beneath a blanket of casseroles and baked goods. Dorena pushed food at her, but the thought of eating was revolting. She shoved her food around on her plate, barely noticing when Mike and Dorena drifted away, to carry on a quiet conversation in the far corner of the crowded room.

Suddenly Keely felt a presence beside her and someone touched her shoulder. She turned, and almost melted at the warm concern in Noah's gray-flannel eyes.

"How are you holding up?" he asked, forking a pickle from the relish dish. "Did you get any sleep?"

"Some."

"Have you seen Todd?" He looked around the room. "He disappeared a few minutes ago."

"It's not my turn to watch out for Todd," she answered, as her partner, Bob Craybill, joined them.

"Hey, partner, how's it going?" he asked, giving her a light kiss. Nodding at Noah, he held out his hand. "You must be Todd's brother. I see the resemblance."

Noah shook his hand and introduced himself. While the two men conversed, Keely found herself studying Noah's face. She didn't see much resemblance to his younger brother. True, they had the same coloring and basic bone structure, but Todd had a boyish quality while Noah had a rigorous, manly look that bespoke experience and sophistication. Noah Bannister had aged well; no doubt he was a very eligible bachelor in his own social circle.

A circle that no longer included Keely.

She wandered over to a group clustered around the dining room table, speaking in self-consciously hushed voices. Keely felt their guilt as she approached. Guilt because their lives were still intact.

Faye Preston, her father's neighbor for nine years, clutched her hand and dragged her to a small love seat in the corner. "Keely, Hank and I are so sorry. I know what you must be feeling and if there's anything we can do..."

Keely patted her hand and nodded. Faye was a good friend. She had so many good friends, she realized, yet she couldn't lighten her load by confiding in any of them. The suspicions she was harboring about her dead sister were just too ugly, too devastating, to share.

When even Faye ran out of comforting words, she excused herself and said something about getting a bite to eat. Keely sat alone on the sofa, staring into space and wondering how she was going to endure this day—not to mention the next week with the insufferable Noah Bannister.

She'd just about reached the decision to call off the entire operation when she was distracted by a familiar voice.

"Hey, partner, why'd you run off and leave me?"

Keely swiveled her head and smiled at Bob Craybill. She reached up and took his hand, guiding him onto the love seat beside her. "I'm sorry. I can't seem to light for very long. I just keep wandering around. How about you, Bob? Haven't had much chance to talk with you in days."

He grimaced and drank deeply from the goblet of wine he was carrying. "I hate funerals almost as much as I hate divorces."

She couldn't help but laugh. "You might be a lot better off if you hated weddings, too!"

"You got a point."

Bob had recently separated from his third wife, and Keely knew that beneath his gruff exterior, he was still hurting. Marriage wasn't easy for any cop, but Bob seemed to make a career out of building relationships then destroying them. As his partner, Keely felt powerless to help him. In some ways, Bob was bent on self-destruction, but it was still painful for a friend to watch.

He took another slug of his wine. "So what's going on? The entire division is buzzing about some secret deal between you and that fed. Care to tell your old partner about it?"

She lowered her gaze and picked a pale thread off her dark skirt. She didn't want to lie to Bob, but his tendency to run his mouth—especially after he'd had a few—left her no alternative.

Keeping her face averted, she murmured, "My business with Noah Bannister is personal. Some old unfinished stuff you'd rather not hear about."

Wordlessly, Bob stood up and walked away. A moment later he reappeared carrying a newly filled wineglass. He took a sip. "Yeah, I heard you and the fed were old high school sweethearts or something. Didn't quite understand why you guys held your love reunion in the chief's office, though."

Keely bit her lip; she wasn't fooling Bob. Still, she'd given her word not to discuss the investigation. "You know the chief's an old family friend, Bob. Noah's known him forever, as well. He came for the funeral and stopped at the chief's office to pay his respects. No big secret."

He drained his glass and stood up. "I guess not. Erma said you guys stayed in his office over two hours. That's a lot of respect, even for old friends."

"Did I hear someone take my name in vain?" Erma Rodriguez's cheery voice chirped.

"Hi, Erma!" Keely gushed, thankful for the diverting presence of the older woman.

Bob leaned over and pecked Keely on the cheek. "Catch you later, partner."

"See you, Bob."

Erma jerked a thumb toward his departing figure. "What's up with him? He's acting even more morose than usual."

Again Keely felt compelled to stretch the truth to its outer bounds. "He's still feeling blue over his latest marital mishap, I think."

Erma nodded sagely. "The man has plenty to be upset about. I heard she's popping for big-time alimony payments."

"Alimony? They were only married a little over a year," Keely protested.

"Maybe so. But the way I heard it, she's claiming she gave up her career to be a full-time wifey, and now Bob should take care of her for life. I guess they don't call it alimony anymore—the politically correct term is spousal support. Of course, in order to get any money, your spouse has to actually hold down a job. Unlike the snake I was married to."

Feeling uneasy about engaging in a touchy subject, Keely shrugged. "I guess the judge will sort it all out."

"Hmmph! More likely the lawyers will be the ones taking all the money home."

The conversation was making Keely increasingly uncomfortable. Everyone knew that when Erma's own long-term marriage ended in divorce, she was left with little more than the roof over her head and five kids to raise. In the intervening years, she'd never ceased grousing about the lawyers and the system stripping her of her rightful due.

Keely glanced around, looking for a plausible excuse to escape. She understood that most people didn't know what to say at a funeral so they either said exactly the wrong thing, or completely ignored the subject; obviously Erma was opting for the latter.

"Keely!"

She looked up to see her father beckoning from the kitchen doorway. "Excuse me a minute, will you, Erma?"

"Sure, honey. You go on and help your father."

Keely smiled and made her escape.

She found Mike Travers in the kitchen talking quietly with Noah. Her heart thumped double-time in automatic reaction to his striking presence.

"What's up, Pop?" she asked quietly as she slipped an arm around her father's painfully thin waist.

"I just heard that you two are going to be taking a vacation this week."

She whirled and glared at Noah. "You had no right to tell my father about this assignment!"

Mike stepped between them. "He didn't tell me. Lyle Kapinski told me off the record. I guess if he hadn't confided in me, I'd just have been left to wonder when you disappeared for a week or so."

Ignoring Noah, Keely reached for her father. Forcing cheer into her voice, she couldn't hide the tremble in her hand as she patted her father's thin arm. He was upset enough over Rosie's death and his own illness; she couldn't heap more worry on him. "I was going to tell you, but I didn't have a chance."

He shrugged off her hand. "What about in the kitchen today? Seems to me we were alone long enough for you to mention this."

"I'm sorry, Pop. I didn't want to upset you."

"Well, I'm upset now. And what'd you mean about an assignment? Lyle gave me the impression that you two were going on a romantic cruise to try and iron out, you know, the past. I want to know what that has to do with an assignment?"

"I, uh, that is, we are going on a cruise. It's part of an investigation Noah's been involved with for quite some time and he asked me—"

"Don't they have female agents in the Treasury Department, Noah?" Mike cut in.

Noah straightened up and stepped forward to join them. "Yes, sir, but Keely was more suited to... she had specialized knowledge about the case."

Mike turned away from Noah and stared hard at his daughter. "This is about Rosie, isn't it?"

She laid her head on his shoulder. "Now, Pop, don't get yourself all worked up. We're not at all sure that Rosie was involved in this case of Noah's." Raising her head, she glared over her father's shoulder, daring Noah to dispute her words.

But Mike wasn't buying her story. "You're a lousy liar, Keely. I don't know how you expect to go undercover when you can't even tell a convincing fib to make an old man feel better. Now if it's just that you don't want to tell me about it—"

"It's not that I don't want to," she interrupted. "But the whole case would be compromised if word leaked. Not that I think you'd tell anyone, but I promised Chief Kapinski that—"

Mike pushed her back and held her at arm's length. His eyes bright with anger, he said, "And you thought that included me? Your father? Hells bells, I guess I must be quite a blabbermouth if my own daughter doesn't trust me!"

"Pop, it's not like that."

Unbending in his anger, he stalked to the doorway. "Have it your way. If you ever decide that I might have the right to know what happened to my youngest child, you know where to find me."

He disappeared into the milling crowd in the dining room.

"Thanks a lot, Noah," she muttered as she stared at her father's retreating back.

"Hey, I'm not the one who leaked word of our assignment—your esteemed boss did. With your help, of course."

She grabbed a glass out of the kitchen cabinet and filled it with tap water. Taking a long swallow, she wiped her mouth with the back of her hand. "That was a slip of the tongue—not a deliberate leak."

Noah shrugged. "Whatever you say. But if we're going to have any chance at all of pulling this off, I'd suggest you watch what you say—even to your own family."

He followed Mike's path into the dining room, leaving Keely alone in the kitchen.

Suddenly she'd had enough. She didn't want to go back into the front of the house and endure more stares and whispers. She didn't want to face Noah's scathing glances and her father's hurt expression. Mike had a hot temper but he always cooled off quickly. Within an hour he'd be back to his old cantankerous self.

She would take longer to heal. Right now Keely didn't want to hear any more departmental gossip, or be the source of more endless speculation. She wanted to be completely alone to sort out her confused feelings.

Grabbing her handbag out of the kitchen desk drawer, she slipped out the back door. Her own car was parked down the street and she hurried along the sidewalk before some well-meaning soul saw her and decided she needed company.

When she was only a few yards from her little red compact, she was startled and dismayed to see Dale Cabot leaning against the fender.

"Dale! What are you doing out here alone? Everyone's inside."

"That's why I'm outside. Crowds make me crazy."

She smiled; at least he wasn't going to be difficult. "Me too. I had to get some air."

He nodded to the keys in her hand. "Where are you going?"

"I thought I'd take a drive. Roll down the windows and let the fresh air clean out the cobwebs."

"Want some company?" He cocked his head and gazed at her, adoration shining in his eyes.

Shaking her head slowly, she took a hesitant step toward the driver's-side door. "Thanks for the offer, but I'd really like to be alone. I'm sure you understand."

He unfolded his long legs and stood with his hands pressed against his hipbones. "Yeah, I understand. I was good enough for company before Noah Bannister came back to town, but now you'd rather spend time alone in a barnyard than a few minutes with me."

Keely's temper snapped. She'd simply been through too much to allow him to indulge in any more self-pity at her expense. "Oh, Dale, knock it off! We had a few dates, that's all. I thought we were friends. Please don't make me change my mind."

"I'm only trying to stop you from making a fool of yourself. Everybody knows Noah Bannister dumped you once. Mark my words, Keely, he'll do it again."

She yanked open her car door and slid behind the wheel. Tears of fury hovered beneath her lids.

Cab followed right behind and bent down, shouting through the window. "You can run away, but you know I'm right, Keely."

She rolled down the window. "Cab, please don't say another word. What happened between Noah and me doesn't concern you in the slightest. You keep saying that you care about me. Well, if you did, you wouldn't pick a fight on the day my sister is buried!"

Color washed from his face, and he became instantly contrite. "Jeez, Keely, I'm sorry. What a jerk." He reached through the open window and grabbed her hand. "Don't leave angry at me. Please. I...I just feel kind of, I don't know, left out today. Please say you'll forgive me."

She felt the anger start to drain as she stared at him. His eyes were wide, and he was nervously gnawing his lower lip. Everyone was on edge, including herself. Maybe she was just taking all of her frustration out on poor Cab.

After all, she should have some empathy for his feelings. Noah dumped her once, totally devastating her. And, in a way, she'd dumped Cab. The least she could do was be a little sensitive to his feelings.

Pulling her hand from his grasp, she patted his forearm. "It's okay, Cab. Really. I'm sorry I blew up at you. Friends?"

He stepped back from the car. "Yeah, friends. Go for your drive."

She turned on the engine and waved as she pulled out.

Driving slowly past her father's house, she felt that same sense of being left out that Cab had mentioned. Was it only loneliness? A sudden awareness of that empty place inside her that should be filled by a spe-

cial man? The man she'd once thought was Noah
Bannister.

When she paused at the stop sign on the corner,
Keely glanced in the rearview mirror. Dale Cabot was
still standing in the street, watching her departure.

She'd been so wrong once about Noah. Was she
making another mistake by dismissing Cab so easily?

The memory of Noah's slate gaze slowly raking over
her was the only answer she needed. If she could still
respond so quickly, so thoroughly, to Noah, she wasn't
ready for a relationship with anyone else.

Chapter Four

Deciding that a long numbing drive was exactly what she needed, Keely took Interstate 8 toward Arizona. She scarcely realized her direction until she saw the exit for Sunrise Highway and knew this had been her destination all along.

She pulled over and stared at the mountainside, now covered with dry summer brush. In the winter the peak was often dusted with snow and it had been a favorite spot of the Travers girls and the Bannister boys.

Rosie, in particular, had loved the snow.

Driving home, Keely wasn't aware how long she had sat, saying her private goodbyes to her sister, but dusk was already creeping over the horizon when she pulled into the driveway.

Thank God, the worst day of my life is over. She sighed. The worst of her pain was subsiding, as well, but Keely felt isolated. And horribly empty.

Opening the trunk, she hauled out the purchases she'd made that morning for the cruise with Noah. Noah. Just sharing the same room with him at her father's house had been disconcerting enough, though dozens of other people were there as insulation. She'd still felt his presence wrap around her like flannel sheets in winter. Soft, warm and easy to get used to.

But his sensual charm wouldn't work its magic on her this time. Now she was older and sadly wiser. This time she'd handle Noah Bannister *and* her own emotions.

Her arms burdened with packages, Keely balanced her purse against the front doorframe while she rummaged for her key. Home. Never had her tiny crackerbox house looked more inviting. Dumping her packages on the bench near the front door, she let her purse slip from her fingers onto the floor and stepped out of her pumps.

So much had happened in the past few days, Keely felt as if she'd been strapped into a roller coaster and forced to ride over and over. Her mind and her emotions were still reeling.

Bone weary, she padded barefoot toward the kitchen, sorting through the mail and flipping on lights. Snagging a couple of bills and discarding the rest, her eye automatically went to her cat's empty food dish. "Malcolm?"

For a moment she was worried when the overpampered and overfed feline didn't waddle in for his evening kibble. Then Keely recalled asking her neighbor to scoop him up and keep him until she returned from Mexico.

Oh, if only she were going to Mexico for a long-deserved vacation. Instead of a sham honeymoon with Noah.

Even as the thought formed, it was quickly negated by the sudden thrill that pulsed in her heart. She put her hand to her chest to still the telltale thumping. She was hungry, that's all. A little light-headed because she had skipped lunch.

Pouring herself a glass of ice tea, she opened the refrigerator to scan the meager contents. What was she going to fix for dinner? Something fast and fortifying. Other than a bagel slathered with cream cheese for breakfast, she hadn't eaten another morsel all day.

Pulling out a few still-edible mushrooms and a stalk of only slightly wilted broccoli, she started throwing together a basic pasta primavera.

While waiting for the water to boil for her noodles, Keely went into the den to check her answering machine. The flashing display showed two messages. She punched the replay button.

"Hi, Keely. This is Dad. I, uh, just wanted to tell you how much I appreciated your taking over for Todd and me. I wish I had your strength, honey. I'm sorry that I...I got in your face today about the...you know, the business."

A sudden lump formed in her throat as she heard her father's genuine sorrow for causing her more pain. In her adult life, her father had never raised his voice to her; it was only stress that had made him overreact today. She knew this phone call was his way of apologizing and she felt a warm surge of love for her taciturn parent.

She heard the faint embarrassment in his tone as the message continued. "Listen, honey, Noah and Todd are coming over for supper tonight. Why don't you come, too? About six." A long pause, as if her father were waiting for her answer, then, "Okay, I guess that's it. Call me, honey."

Keely ignored the invitation while she waited for the second message.

"Keely? Bob Craybill here. Hey, I didn't get much chance to talk to you after the funeral. I guess I'd had a little too much to drink at your dad's house."

She smiled. This, too, was Bob's way of apologizing for being so invasive and abrupt. After a pause, his voice continued, "So, uh, what's going on? I got your memo and...hey, rumors are flying all over the place."

Her smile widened as she imagined Bob's chagrin at being so close to the source of the latest gossip, yet not knowing any juicy details.

"Anyway, why don't you give me a ring tonight? I'd really like to talk to you."

I bet you would, she mused, not bothering to jot down his home number.

She was about to walk away when the phone rang, its shrill signal startling and intrusive in the quiet. For a moment she hesitated. The day had been too draining already; she wasn't ready to deal with more awkward condolences.

Still, her years of training as a peace officer wouldn't allow her to ignore the continued ringing. With a sigh of resignation, she lifted the receiver. "Hello?"

A heavy silence greeted her.

Raising her voice slightly, she tried again, "Hello? Is anyone there?"

Finally a male voice whispered in her ear, "Keely Travers? Did you have a rough day, Keely?"

"Who is this?" She cocked her head, trying without success to identify the voice. It had a muffled quality, as if the speaker were faraway.

His words, however, were startlingly clear. "I have a message for you, Keely Travers. It was too bad your sister couldn't follow the program. She paid with her life. Don't make the same mistake. This is the only warning you'll get.''

She waited, breathlessly, for more, but a soft click was followed by the dial tone. Her caller had hung up.

She held on to the receiver and mentally replayed the brief conversation. Again. And again. Then, without thinking, she slammed the receiver into the cradle as if she could somehow smash away the ugly, whispered voice forever.

But she couldn't erase the vile words from her mind. An ugly, icy fear started in the pit of her stomach and trickled through her veins. Who was this man? Had he issued a warning or a threat? Or both?

What did he mean, about Rosie paying ''with her life''?

Had he meant that her sister's death hadn't been accidental?

The quickening fear in her heart wouldn't be denied. Rosie had been murdered. But why? How?

Fighting against the surge of nausea in her throat, Keely breathed deeply, ordering control back into her trembling body. After a moment she pulled her hand from her mouth, barely aware of the throbbing pain where she'd bitten herself.

Arms clamped protectively around herself, Keely stumbled back to the kitchen and unlocked the back door. She was suffocating; she had to get some air. Rushing outside, she sagged against the trunk of her favorite jacaranda and tried to force air into her lungs. *Breathe, Keely, breathe.*

Slowly, she felt the flow of blessed air fill her chest. Huddled against the tree trunk, she once again tried to absorb the horrifying message. Rosie, murdered?

Unable to bear the thought, Keely felt tears of despair trickle down her cheekbones.

"Keely?"

"Oh!" She jumped and spun around.

Noah Bannister's tall, solid form stood inches behind her. Even in her distress Keely wondered how he had managed to creep up so quietly. What was he doing there in the first place?

Taking a step forward, he clasped her shoulders. "You're trembling! What's wrong?"

Feeling the well of tears about to spring forth, she pointed toward the house and mumbled, "My sister was killed because—" She broke off as a sob caught in her throat. She wouldn't let Noah see her fall apart.

He stared for a long moment. When he spoke, his voice remained cool and unemotional. "Are you saying that Rosie was deliberately killed?"

Squaring her shoulders, she nodded.

With a deep, shuddering sigh, he pulled her close, nestling her damp face against his chest. His large hands stroked the top of her head, ruffling her short-cropped hair. After a moment Keely's shock began to subside, as if she had somehow drawn strength from Noah's calmness.

"Come on," he whispered against her hair, "let's go inside."

By the time they returned to the kitchen, where Keely drank deeply from a revitalizing glass of water, she felt almost back in control. She turned to find Noah leaning against the counter, staring at her with his impenetrable smoky gaze. Keely took refuge behind the table.

"Are you all right now?"

She nodded.

"Can you start at the beginning? What makes you think Rosie was murdered?"

Murdered. The word hung suspended, like the blade of a guillotine, menacing and dreadful.

Seeing her falter, Noah moved to join her at the table and leaned over the scarred wooden top, focusing his full attention on Keely. The incredible strength of his presence filled the small kitchen. He was too near and too potent for comfort. With his nearness, she suddenly realized he'd never mentioned why he'd been prowling around her yard in the first place.

"Keely?" he prodded.

"Oh! It was really dreadful. First Dad, then Bob Craybill. And...oh, I don't mean them. It was the third call—" She stopped abruptly, unable to continue. Noah's close scrutiny only intensified the strain on her already frayed nerves.

Noah had known Keely Travers most of his life. True, he hadn't seen her for almost ten years, but she couldn't have changed this much. She'd always been confident to the point of foolhardiness; now she seemed hesitant and way too vulnerable. Something had frightened her, badly frightened her.

Suddenly an acrid odor assailed his nose and Noah pointed toward the stove. "What are you burning over there? That pot's turning red."

Keely whirled around. Damn! She'd forgotten all about the water she'd put on for her pasta before she listened to her messages. Noah hadn't been exaggerating; the pan was completely empty and red hot.

Grabbing oven mitts, she raced to the stove and yanked the pot off the burner. She dropped it into the sink and turned on the water, which enveloped it in a haze of hissing steam. The burnt pan was the final straw. Too much had happened in too short a period and Keely's ability to cope abandoned her.

She stood there, steam and spray hitting her face until Noah came up behind her and shut off the tap.

Guiding her by the shoulders, he led her to the table and gently pushed her into a chair. Sitting down across from her again, he said quietly, "You seem pretty strung out. I know Rosie's death is certainly part of it, but this afternoon you seemed as if you were handling it. So what's happened since then? What's got you so spooked?"

Keely looked up, her face pale and haunted. She reached across the table and clasped his hand tightly, the intensity in her gaze compelling him to take her seriously. "My sister's death was no accident, Noah. There's no doubt in my mind that it had something to do with this counterfeiting scheme."

"You said that outside, but why haven't you mentioned it before? What makes you believe the crash wasn't an accident?"

Keely raked her fingers through her shaggy black bob. "Tonight I received a phone call. He said he had a ... a message for me."

He frowned. "What kind of message?"

Keely tersely repeated the coldly whispered speech. She had no fear of leaving anything out; the hateful words had been burned into her brain like a cattle brand.

Noah stared at her for a long time, as if gauging her objectivity. "And you didn't recognize the voice?"

"No. Only that I'm sure it was male. I've thought of everyone I know and can't get a match. Yet ... yet it sounded familiar. Almost as if the caller was trying to disguise his voice. Talking through a scarf or something.''

He gave her a curious look. ''Are you sure you're okay?''

She pushed back her chair and eyed him balefully. ''Just because I had a shock doesn't mean I'm ready for a rubber room. Of course I'm okay. Sort of.''

''Sorry. No slur intended.''

''Then stop patronizing me.''

Ignoring her accusation, he drummed his fingertips on the tabletop for a few seconds. ''I don't think we can write this off as a crank call.''

Keely nodded. ''I know. There was something horribly... sincere about the way he uttered that threat. I've never heard such a cold-blooded message in my life, and after working vice for two years, believe me, I've heard a lot!''

''Maybe. But, trust me, working vice in a laid-back city like San Diego is a far cry from—''

She leapt to her feet. ''If you're trying to tell me that my professional experience can't equal what you've learned in the big, bad city, then let me tell you something, Mr. Hotshot Bannister. I—''

He held up his hands to stem the flow of her words. ''That isn't what I meant at all, Keely, so stop trying to put words in my mouth.''

She crossed her arms and deliberately fastened her gaze on her empty water glass.

''Look,'' Noah continued, after a long, tension-filled pause. ''I know we've got a lot of unresolved history, but we've also got a tough week coming up. Since we're going to be in such close proximity, how about we call a truce until this case is over. Deal?'' He reached across the table, extending his hand.

Keely knew he was right. But she didn't know if she could put the past aside as easily as Noah. Of course, he'd left her with the broken heart—not the other way around. Still, she prided herself on being a law-enforcement professional and she wasn't going to give him any reason to say otherwise. If he could bury the past, then so would she.

"Deal." She accepted his handshake but couldn't stop herself from putting a little extra force in her grasp.

Instead of responding to the enthusiasm of her handshake, he picked up the thread of their earlier conversation. "So that's everything that's happened, right? You haven't left anything out?"

In reply she shrugged her shoulders. What she hadn't revealed were her own doubts. Why was Noah spearheading this investigation? Surely someone else in his department could have handled the assignment. He must have known how unsettling his presence would be.

He'd hinted to Chief Kapinski that there was a leak in the San Diego PD. But what if that leak was higher up? Maybe in the Treasury Department itself? What if Noah Bannister had returned to his hometown to protect his cover?

As soon as he arrived, Keely had received a threatening phone call. A mere coincidence? Maybe, but who else knew of her involvement? Who else was afraid she would be a threat to the counterfeiters?

There was one question she couldn't ignore any longer. "Why were you in my yard earlier? Why did you come over in the first place?"

He leaned back in his chair, his gaze fastened on the ceiling. "Two reasons. First, your dad sent me. He said I was to bring you to his place for dinner. My mom cooked a ham and there's all those leftovers from the wake.''

Keely blinked in disbelief. Surely Mike would realize how painful it would be for Keely to spend the evening with Noah, as if they were all one big happy family.

And Noah. Had he taken leave of his senses? Did he really believe that ten years could be swept aside without a word of explanation or apology?

Slowly, Keely rose to her feet. ''Thanks for coming, Noah. I appreciate your help.''

He rubbed his fingers through the enticing darkness along his jawline and shook his head. ''I'm worried about your caller. He might show up to give you the message in person.''

''Then I guess I'll have to show him my badge and ask him to leave,'' she replied, sarcasm dripping from her voice.

Ignoring her tone, he continued, ''If you can spare a blanket and pillow, I can camp out on the sofa.''

Anger started burbling in her veins again. So Mr. Macho didn't think she was capable of taking care of herself? By treating her like a helpless victim, he was impugning her skills as a seasoned police officer. ''Good idea, Noah. If my caller shows up, you can show him *your* badge. Maybe it's shinier than mine and will scare him more. Please tell my father I couldn't make dinner.''

Still resting comfortably with his long legs propped on the edge of the table, his chair tilted on its two back legs, Noah raised his gaze to meet hers. ''What's the matter, Keely? Too proud to break bread with me?''

Clasping the back of her own chair until her fingers were white with the effort, she forced a firmness into her voice that didn't match the wobbly sensation in her stomach. "Quite frankly, Noah, I'd rather break bread with the devil than share a meal with you."

Slowly rising to his feet, he tucked his fingertips into the back pockets of his snug jeans. Offering a brief, rare flash of his dimpled grin, he said, "Then I'd say our honeymoon should be quite interesting. The idea of lazing around on a cruise ship for the next week wasn't too exciting. Now I'm kind of looking forward to those long nights in our stateroom."

Those same long nights she dreaded like the plague.

Noah cocked his head and stared into her eyes. "I really don't like the idea of your being alone tonight. Please let me stay."

Keely's chin jutted upward. "In addition to four years of self-defense training, I have at my disposal a telephone, a police baton, a canister of mace and a stun gun. I also have two handguns and three rifles in the house. Thanks for the offer all the same, but I think I can manage."

As he sauntered to the back door, he said over his shoulder, "Suit yourself. By the way, you never did ask me about reason number two."

"Number two?"

"Yeah, my other reason for coming over here tonight."

"So what is it?" she asked, wishing he would hurry up and leave.

He stopped and dug in the pocket of his jeans. "To give you this. I figured if we're going to be married for a week, you'd need it." He slipped a tiny object into her palm and closed her fingers around it.

Slowly unfolding her fingers, she stared in astonishment at the small golden circle. "It—it's a wedding ring."

"My grandmother's. She gave it to me back when it looked as if you and I were— Anyway, she always wanted you to have it, so it's yours."

She looked up, locking gazes with this man who both troubled and delighted her so. "Noah, I can't accept this. It wouldn't be right."

He shrugged. "If you don't want it, give it to charity, sell it, throw it away. I don't care. I just thought that a married woman would wear a ring of some kind."

She slipped the gold band on her ring finger. It fit as if it had been custom-designed for her. "It's lovely, Noah. Thank you."

With an arch of his eyebrows, he nodded and opened the back door. "Be sure and lock the door behind me. I wouldn't want anything to happen to my lovely bride."

LATER THAT NIGHT, Keely snapped the front-door dead bolt into place and turned off the overhead light in the foyer. She was so tired, so utterly exhausted, she considered grabbing an afghan out of the closet and camping out on the sofa rather than face that flight of stairs. But the thought of her own comfy bed was too alluring.

Besides, she needed to hoard all the quality sleep she could garner. Noah was picking her up early in the morning for the two-plus-hour drive to the dock at

Long Beach. And she still had to pack, which meant getting up at least an hour earlier.

She trudged up the steps, ruing whatever foolish notion had made her agree to this madcap idea in the first place. Faking a honeymoon with Noah—absurd. What had she been thinking?

In the bathroom she gave her face a quick rinse and scrubbed her teeth. Looking in the mirror, she was startled to see the image that greeted her. The dark circles beneath her eyes were incongruous with the short, sassy hairdo.

As she smoothed on a layer of cold cream, she prayed that Noah was wrong and that the call had only been a sick prank. Nothing to worry about.

After all, if Rosie had been an innocent bystander, as Keely believed, no one had any reason to harm her. And she desperately clung to her faith in her sister's innocence.

A few minutes later she climbed into bed, pulled the lightweight cotton spread up over her shoulders and willed sleep to claim her. But her mind was too busy, sorting and reliving fragments of the day, most of them involving Noah.

Keely turned over and plumped her pillow. *Sleep, think about sleep,* she chided herself. But the blessed comfort of slumber continued to elude her.

It was in the dark, eerie hours well past midnight, and Keely was still tossing and twisting in her bed when the phone beside her shrilled.

Her first thought was her father. The cancer and its treatments had already taken a terrible toll on his strength. Had the stress of losing his youngest daughter pushed Pop out of remission?

With a fearful hand, Keely picked up the receiver. "Hello?"

"Keely Travers?"

Cold chills washed up her spine at the deep, raspy voice. The same vaguely familiar voice that had called earlier. Hoping her alarm didn't echo in her voice, she said sharply, "Who are you? What do you want?"

His reply was a throaty chuckle. "I like you, Keely, so I thought I'd make sure you understood the importance of my first message. Isn't it funny, Detective, how deaths seem to come in threes? Since there's already been two, I'd be very careful if I were you. Very careful."

Before she could find her voice, the line was disconnected.

Shaken by the sound of that malevolent voice, she dropped the receiver and eased out of bed. Keely crossed the room and took her service revolver from its holster.

She tiptoed back and laid the gun on her bedside table and climbed beneath the covers, feeling only slightly more secure with her weapon close at hand.

Despite the caller's attempt to disguise his voice, the cadence of his speech, the very manner in which he formed his sentences sounded familiar. Too familiar. Yet she couldn't place it.

Keely bit her lip, knowing deep in her heart the caller wasn't a crank, or even a stranger. He was somebody she knew and maybe even trusted.

And he'd threatened to kill her.

Chapter Five

"Look," Noah said, casting a sidelong glance at Keely, who was sitting huddled against the passenger door, "I think we ought to use this time driving to Long Beach to clear the air between us."

Keely's chin lifted and her jaw tightened. "Frankly, I don't have the least interest in discussing the past."

"Come on, Keely. I never should have left like I did without saying a word. I've regretted that for years. I should have at least said goodbye."

She sighed, deeply and heavily. "Okay, fine. You're forgiven. Can we forget the ancient history now?"

"What are you so hot about?"

"Nothing," she snapped. "I just think our time could be better spent figuring out a plan for once we're on the ship. What exactly are we looking for—or whom? How are we going to know our quarry if we stumble over them? And what do we do about it?"

"Keely, quit changing the subject. We need to—"

She wheeled around in her seat and faced him. "There is no 'we,' Noah! There hasn't been in ten years. We had a brief high school romance. It's over. Life goes on. If your conscience won't leave you alone, I'm sorry, but we all have our little regrets. Now, can we use this time to lay out the groundwork for this investigation?''

Noah rapped the steering wheel with his palm and gritted his teeth. Keely had always known how to push his buttons, and it was obvious that time hadn't diminished her insight. She knew it would bug him to leave this matter unresolved.

What Keely didn't understand was that *his* conscience wasn't bothering him, although her own conscience should be throbbing like hell. She was the one who had been responsible for the disintegration of their relationship, not him. It was her lack of trust, her hurled accusations, that had pierced his heart like a sword thrust. That was why he'd fled San Diego to spend his college years living with a cousin in San Francisco. Not once, not a single time did she attempt to contact him.

He knew because eventually he'd weakened and told his mother to let Keely know where he was—if she asked. Apparently she never did.

Well, if she couldn't own up to her responsibility for their tattered past, far be it from him to push the matter. He'd thought clearing the air would make it easier for them to work together. If she only wanted to talk about the case for the next week, then so be it. He wouldn't utter a single personal word. Noah knew how to play hardball, as Keely would quickly discover.

"All right," he said at last, "we'll play it your way. Strictly business." He paused again and cleared his throat. Damn the woman—it sure hadn't taken her long to get under his skin again. But she wasn't going to manipulate him, not this time. Keeping his voice carefully neutral, he continued, "I think someone will be on this cruise to check us out. Since the police still haven't located Sargent's next of kin, I think there's a very good chance that news of his death hasn't filtered to his associates yet."

"What about the newspapers?"

He frowned. "There was only the one fairly brief article on the local page. I seriously doubt a two-person, single-car accident would have made the wire services."

"What about the leak in the police department you were talking about? If there is an informant, wouldn't he pass word of Sargent's death to the syndicate back East?"

Noah nodded. "That's certainly a possibility. On the other hand, I think it's unlikely that the contact in Mexico has received the word."

Keely raised a delicately arched black eyebrow. "Even in this age of faxes and cellular phones?"

"Faxes and cellular phones could certainly play a part in this equation. We could be walking into a trap. It isn't too late to back out, you know. I could get another agent from the Los Angeles branch to pose as Rosie."

Keely twisted in the seat and stared at him. "Yesterday you said I was the only one who could pull this off. What happened to change your mind?"

He sucked on his upper lip as he negotiated a tight squeeze through the bumper-to-bumper traffic. "What happened was that phone call. By hinting that Rosie and Sargent were murdered, your caller raised the ante."

"You're worried about me," she said, a hint of awe coloring her tone.

He turned his head and stared out the side window before returning his attention to the road ahead.

"Look, this is my job, not yours. I should never have involved you."

"But you did," she countered. "If we know up front that we might be walking into a trap, we'll be better prepared. More cautious." When he started to interrupt, her voice rose to cover his. "I'm in for the long haul now, Noah. There's one thing about me you never realized. I'm not a quitter."

Like you were, hung unspoken in the air between them.

After a few tense seconds, he shrugged. "It really doesn't matter. If they know about Rosie and Sargent and the transfer is off, the contact won't be on the ship and the courier won't show up in Ensenada."

"I guess you're right," she said slowly, as if trying to find a hole in his logic. Finally she nodded to herself and said, "Okay, so we proceed on the assumption that our cover is intact. We're Rosie and Todd Bannister, on our honeymoon—"

"No," he interrupted. "I think we should stick with our own first names. Otherwise there'll be confusion between our passports and what we're calling ourselves."

"Won't the contact expect Rosie and Todd?"

"I looked those tickets over pretty carefully. They only say Mr. and Mrs. Bannister. I think we'll be fine."

"Good," she said, and leaned back in the seat. She closed her eyes as if she'd fallen asleep, but Noah could see the uneven pulse thrumming in her throat and knew she was awake.

What was she thinking? Was she, perhaps, reliving the past and wishing for a different future than the one they'd each made for themselves?

"KEELY? WAKE UP. We're at the pier."

Sitting up with a start, she rubbed her eyes and stared out the windshield in surprise. Right in front of them was the magnificent ocean liner, *Empress of the Seas*. What an incredible sight! Vast, majestic and bobbing calmly at the dock like a dowager queen. The vessel was pristine white except for a wide blue stripe where the ship's hull curved inward. Marine blue lifeboats were fastened along one of the decks. Multicolored nautical flags draped the *Empress* from her elegant bow, up to the top of the superstructure and down again, ending at the stern.

"I never imagined it would be so huge," Keely breathed.

Noah opened the car door, slid out and stretched his travel-weary limbs. "Well, she's going to be our home for the next week. Let's hope the old gal is watertight."

Keely stepped around to the rear of the car to help Noah carry their suitcases on board. Impatiently waving off her offer, he hoisted the bags and led the way toward the gangplank, where they could see other passengers already embarking.

The loading process was fast and efficient. After joining a line inside the terminal marked A To L, they handed their luggage, passports and cruise tickets to a cheery clerk dressed in red, white and blue. Five minutes later they were heading up a long concrete walkway that terminated at the ship's gangway.

Keely's first surprise came when they reached the top of the ramp. A ship's officer, nattily attired in sparkling white, stepped up to greet them. "Welcome aboard, folks." He glanced at the boarding package given to them by the terminal clerk. "Ah, you've

booked one of our honeymoon cabins. We'll try our
best to make your stay as romantic as possible," he
concluded with a meaningful wink. "Okay, folks, time
for that first photo opportunity."

Following his direction, they stood beside a large
cardboard sign, gaily painted with the ship's name and
the inscription Mexican Cruise.

"Come on, folks, you're newlyweds—you can stand
closer than that!"

Keely groaned inwardly. It was starting already. She
wanted to scream at the man that she couldn't stand
any closer to Noah, else she'd lose her breath completely. Noah, seemingly oblivious to her discomfort,
pulled her close in a pseudoloving embrace and
mugged for the camera. Finally the shutter snapped
and she was able to pull away.

The man who'd been their official greeter handed
their tickets to another white-suited man who introduced himself as Manny and informed them he would
be their cabin steward for the trip. Charming and
knowledgeable, Manny rattled off the ship's vital sta-
tistics and history as he led them to their cabin.

Pausing at a short, curved portal, he pointed to a
four-inch-high iron plate at the bottom of the doorframe. "Watch your step here. Don't want to trip over
this water guard."

They entered a small vestibule, closed off from the
main living quarters by a sliding curtain. Pulling the
privacy curtain aside, Manny led the way into the
compact living space and demonstrated the various
accoutrements. After explaining the flushing system
in the tiny bathroom, and the mechanism that con-
verted the sofa into a room-size bed, he smiled
brightly. "So, how long you been married?"

"Three weeks," Keely answered.

"Six months," Noah said at the same time.

Keely gulped. Obviously they should have spent their time refining their cover story instead of arguing. She laughed wryly and tucked her arm through Noah's. "It only *seems* like six months, darling."

They both treated the steward to dazzling smiles.

Manny stepped back and raised an eyebrow. "Uh-huh. Well, none of my business, that's for sure. Now, the bar won't open until after the captain's lifeboat drill, sometime soon after we set sail." Manny showed them how to don their life jackets and where to muster when the drill was announced.

Then he pulled their tickets out of his pocket and studied them for a moment. "You've been assigned to the second seating in the Bahia Harbor dining room. That's on D Deck. They'll announce it over the loudspeaker. May I do anything else for you right now?"

"No, that'll be fine," Noah said, reaching into his pocket.

Manny held up his hand. "Oh, no, sir. Gratuities are made at the end of the cruise." He glanced at Keely. "I guess you'll want to be alone now, but the captain gets real crabby if anyone misses his emergency drills."

"We won't miss it," Noah said, closing the door firmly behind the little man.

He turned around to face Keely. "Well, *honey,* looks like we're alone. At last."

"Since we are, *darling,* maybe we ought to get our stories straight."

He winked and flopped onto the bed. "No problem, *sweetums.* You lie and I'll swear to it."

THE *EMPRESS*'S immense engines shuddered as they began their warm-up for the long voyage, and Keely released a breath of pent-up frustration. Finally. Thanks to Noah's cold demeanor, the atmosphere in the small stateroom was tense and silent. It was going to be a long, awkward week.

Noah pulled off his sneakers and tucked a bolster pillow behind his neck. "That was a long drive. Think I'll take a little nap before dinner."

He closed his eyes and, true to his word, a few moments later his softly resonant snore filled the cabin.

Unaccountably annoyed, Keely stalked around the confines of the cabin like a wild creature unused to close quarters. She flipped on the television to find only one single working channel, which was running an endless sequence of tide tables and ocean currents.

She snapped it off and peeked through the porthole. The deck chairs outside the window were quickly filling with other passengers so she decided to go on deck and watch the departure preparations.

Taking her electronic door key, she slipped out of the room. Although by now the deck was rapidly filling with other vacationers, Keely managed to find an empty lounge chair tucked in the corner beside an air shaft.

Keely leaned back, adjusted her sunglasses and watched the smiling couples lining the rail as they laughed and waved to well-wishers standing on the dock two stories below. Some had even brought rolls of paper streamers and confetti and were tossing them to the cheering crowd.

The atmosphere was partylike, full of chatter and gaiety. Yet as the multitudes of strangers jostled past, she found herself eyeing them with suspicion. Noah and Chief Kapinski both believed the courier was going to be on this ship.

With millions of dollars of phony money at stake, she knew these people could be ruthless. Perhaps her sister had already fallen prey to their crimes.

If so, there was little doubt she and Noah were going to be closely watched. She looked up and caught the eye of a young crew member straightening deck chairs. How long had he been watching her? Was his interest purely professional, or did his smile hide a darker agenda?

The young man walked toward her. She stiffened in her seat as she watched his approach with trepidation. When he reached her, he merely smiled, tipped his cap and continued down the deck, whistling a sea chanty as he passed.

She laughed nervously. It was one thing to be watchful, but another to be paranoid. This was a cruise; people were always friendlier on vacation. Keely vowed to maintain some equilibrium.

Forcing herself to relax, she leaned back and affably watched her fellow passengers.

A small group strolled past her deck chair, each young couple with fingers entwined, as one woman shared a funny story about her recent wedding. Everyone was laughing and another woman launched into her own tale as they drifted past.

Everywhere Keely looked, happy couples laughed and touched with the shared intimacy of love.

She had never felt more alone in her life. Why, oh why, had she ever agreed to come on this sham honeymoon?

Then there was a long, deep blare of a horn from somewhere on board and the massive liner started moving with surprising speed out of Long Beach Harbor.

Suddenly she felt a presence at her side, but she had no sense of danger. Shielding her eyes from the bright sunlight with the edge of her hand, she looked up. Noah was standing beside her.

"Come on," he said, extending his hand. "Let's join the others and watch the ship leave the harbor. It's traditional," he added when she failed to move.

For a brief instant Keely had felt a flare of hope that he'd come to share this special moment with her because . . . because he wanted to. It was a bitter realization to discover Noah was still in character, playing the role of attentive husband. A role he'd shunned in life.

How could she have ever believed, hoped even, that he fostered some slight regret for what he'd given up? Noah Bannister was cold and uncaring to his core, and she'd do well to keep that knowledge foremost in her mind. He was a man on a mission, nothing more. He wanted to nail this counterfeiting ring and was willing to go to any lengths to achieve his goal.

Keely knew she had to assume the same professional demeanor if she was to survive this assignment with both her heart and her self-respect intact.

Raising her hand to his, she smiled tightly. "Of course, *darling*. I heard someone say the sun would be setting soon off the bow. That'll be so romantic. Shall we?"

Nodding to their fellow passengers, they were still strolling around the deck an hour later. Land was but a faint glimmer on the horizon when the public address system crackled and Captain Jorgensen announced commencement of the first lifeboat drill. Following a flood of passengers, they wordlessly made their way back to their cabin in order to retrieve their life jackets before mustering at their appointed stations on deck.

They suited up in moments. While Noah fiddled with a tangled-up nylon strap at Keely's collar, his warm fingertips grazed the sensitive flesh at her nape and she shuddered involuntarily. "It's only a drill," he assured her, mistaking her reaction. "You'll be fine. I promise."

Recalling her earlier resolve, she snapped, "We both know what your promises are worth."

"Ah, I see. I'm not supposed to make any reference to our checkered past, but you're free to throw barbs whenever the mood strikes. Is that the way we're going to play it?"

Keely flushed. He was right, of course. She had been the one to set up the ground rules; if she expected Noah to follow them, she'd better stick to the plan herself. "I apologize," she said stiffly. "We'd better get to our drill station."

She swept past him out the door.

When they reached the deck, an officer was waiting to direct them to their places in line. Women were sent to the front near the rail; men were packed tightly against the bulkhead.

Keely was given a spot in the last row of women. Directly behind her a narrow walkway was kept clear and then the four rows of men started. As several hundred passengers trooped by, Keely lost sight of Noah. Looking over her shoulder, she caught a glimpse of his gleaming brown hair four rows behind her.

A short dark man wearing a white uniform festooned with lots of gold braid stepped out in front, clipboard in hand. Shouting to make himself heard, he urged everyone to squeeze closer and make room for latecomers.

Keely was already pretty well squashed, she thought, but inched forward until her toes almost touched the heels of the woman in front of her. Still, people continued to crowd down the walkway behind her until it seemed every single one of the sixteen hundred passengers on board must have trooped past.

The man with the clipboard gestured for attention and began giving them emergency instructions. "Now, I'm going to call out your cabin numbers and..."

While he talked, another clump of people came through the nearby door and were edging past her when Keely felt a sharp tug on the strap of her life vest. Before she could react, she was pulled backward a few inches and someone pressed close against her until she could feel hot breath whirling around the back of her neck.

"Hello, Mrs. Bannister," a strange voice whispered. "Make sure you follow directions very carefully. You don't want to fall overboard."

Then the tension on her life jacket eased abruptly. Keely whirled around and stared at the backs of the group who had just passed. Men and women, young and old. Nothing to set any of them apart.

Except one of them had just issued a warning.

Their quarry knew they had arrived and was already one up on them. Noah and Keely had been identified and acknowledged.

The cat-and-mouse game had begun.

Chapter Six

"You're not certain if it was a man or a woman?" Noah asked as they were walking to dinner.

"How many times do I have to answer that? It all happened so fast. Whoever it was jerked my life vest, whispered in my ear and disappeared."

Noah reached around her shoulder to push open the glass door into the Bahia Harbor dining room. As he did so, he drank in the sweetly intoxicating perfume she'd dabbed in a few highly effective spots.

Actually, between the perfume and the red silk dress that whispered over her soft curves like a lover's promise, Noah was having a hard time keeping his mind on the case.

Of course, Keely usually helped him out of his dilemma by biting his head off every third time she spoke to him. Maybe she'd be more civilized after she'd eaten. "I guess we should be grateful," he continued. "At least we're forewarned. The contact is on board so the transfer must be going ahead as scheduled."

He paused as a scarlet-jacketed maître d' glided up to them. "Good evening sir, madame. Your name please?"

"Bannister. Mrs. and Mrs. Bannister."

The maître d' consulted a large seating chart. "Right this way, please."

He led them along a peacock-colored carpet etched with a forest-green-and-navy paisley print. The immense room was dotted with large round tables decked with snowy tablecloths and intricately folded napkins in vivid teal and deep green. Tiny faceted crystal votive candles and fresh flowers completed the decor. Everything was elegant and understated, like the finest gourmet restaurant in a large, cosmopolitan city.

Pausing by a table near the window, which promised a stunning sea view in daylight, the maître d' pulled out a chair for Keely and draped her napkin across her lap. "Fernando will be your waiter for the entire cruise and these lovely people will be your dining companions. I'll leave you to introduce yourselves. Shall I send over the sommelier, sir?"

"Yes, please," Noah replied as he slid into place beside Keely.

After the maître d' departed, he turned to casually study their tablemates. "Good evening. Noah and Keely Bannister here, and you are ... ?"

The middle-aged man to Noah's immediate left extended his hand. "Hebert here. Willie and Florence. From Boise."

"Boise?" Noah arched an eyebrow. "That's a long way."

Florence Hebert leaned forward, resting her sturdy forearms on the table top. "We're celebrating our anniversary. Thirty years."

"Congratulations," Noah and Keely chimed in unison.

Willie's head bobbed emphatically. "This trip was a present from our son. He's a dentist."

"Such a blessing that boy," Florence said. "Tommy never gave us a moment's worry."

"That's great," Noah interjected, before Florence Hebert pulled out photos of the grandkids. Turning his gaze to the next couple in order, he asked, "And you folks?"

This time it was the wife who answered. "Nice to meet you. I'm Beth Gregg and this is my husband, Steve. We're from Orange County."

Noah recognized the name of the affluent suburb of Los Angeles. The Greggs were considerably younger than the Heberts, probably in their mid to late twenties, same as he and Keely.

The blunt-featured man who was seated to Beth Gregg's left rose stiffly to his feet. When he stood up, Noah was surprised to see how immense the man was. Easily six-four and 250 pounds. Noah found himself warily eyeing the huge man; he could be a formidable foe. "Vee are Dieter and Maya Olstagen," he boomed as he thrust out his hand.

Noah did his best to conceal a grimace when Dieter's enormous hand clamped around his. He did notice, however, that Dieter was exceedingly careful when he took Keely's hand, grasping it almost gingerly.

"Are you from Germany?" Keely asked.

"*Nein*—no. We are Swiss," Maya Olstagen responded in a much less accented voice than her husband. She was a sweet-faced woman with sleek blond hair and a slightly buxom figure. A Teutonic beauty.

As he watched the adoring look that Dieter cast upon his lovely wife, Noah was reminded of the legend of Beauty and the Beast.

Conversation was halted while the wine steward took their orders. Then Fernando approached and distributed extravagant dinner menus.

After wine was poured, toasts were offered and the eight strangers set about the business of finding common ground. Willie Hebert was a supervisor at a sock factory in Boise. His wife Florence was a homemaker who spent her free time doing needle crafts.

Steve Gregg was a firefighter, and his wife, Beth, a fifth-grade schoolteacher. They were also celebrating an anniversary, Steve informed them shyly. They'd been married two years.

Now that the ice was broken, the table talk was lively and continuous. While Keely carried the conversational ball, Noah was free to covertly scrutinize their companions. Florence and Willie, Steve and Beth and the Olstagens—all seemingly innocent couples readying for a sun-filled week at sea. Yet Noah's instincts, well honed from his years as a special investigator, fairly shrieked in warning.

The contact was on board, they knew that much for certain. It only made sense that whoever had been sent to keep an eye on them would want to be as close as possible. That made their dining companions prime suspects.

Nor could he rule out Manny, their room steward, or Fernando. Then there were the short-term friends everyone made on vacation. Any of them could be their quarry. He and Keely would have to keep their guard up and not slip out of character for a single moment.

"*Und* you, Herr Bannister?" Dieter Olstagen asked. "What kind of work do you and Mrs. Bannister do?"

There was a sudden stillness as Noah realized they had forgotten to concoct a unified background. He'd taken it for granted that they would assume Todd and Rosie's identity as much as possible. Trouble was, he didn't have the faintest idea what Rosie had done for a living, or if she even worked outside the home at all.

He started to fabricate a story, but Keely smoothly filled the silence.

"I'm a free-lance jewelry designer and Noah is the manager of a Computerland store in San Diego."

Manager? He'd thought Todd was a salesman. Todd never told him he'd been promoted. Then again, how often did he talk to his younger brother? With a guilty start, Noah realized how much distance he'd let drift between himself and those he cared about.

"A computer store!" Florence exclaimed. "I've been wanting to learn how to operate one. Is it very hard, Mr. Bannister?"

"Call me Noah, please," he said with an inward groan. "Check with your local computer store. Most offer lessons." He hoped his terse response would quell any further questions about his "job." His cover would be blown for sure if any of their companions asked his advice for their malfunctioning PCs. Around the office, Noah had the reputation of being "road kill" on the information highway.

Fortunately, conversation again lagged as Fernando arrived with their appetizers and didn't pick up again until after dessert.

While the busboy cleared the dessert and coffee dishes, Willie Hebert leaned back in his chair and patted his stomach. "Whew! That was some feed, all right. I don't know about anybody else, but if I don't walk off some of this grub, I won't sleep a wink tonight."

There were general murmurs of agreement.

Taking the lead, Florence slung her evening bag over her shoulder and stood. "Well, the rest of you can walk around the deck if you want, but I'm heading for the casino! Anybody else game? How about you, Keely, Noah? You guys up for a little blackjack?"

"No, I don't gamble," Keely said. A stricken look on her face, she blurted, "At least, I don't gamble this late at night. I'm an early-to-bed type of gal."

Noah hoped his face didn't betray his thoughts. Rosie had been a gambler—that's how she'd gotten into this mess in the first place. Keely had almost blown their cover—if the syndicate contact was one of their dinner party, anyway. Still, she'd made a nice recovery. With any luck, her slip of the tongue wouldn't be noticed.

Rising to his feet, Noah rushed to pull back her chair. Giving the others a broad wink, he said, "Hey, folks, we're on our honeymoon. I doubt we'll be spending our evenings in the casino, isn't that right, honey?"

She reached up and gave him a none-too-gentle love pat on his cheek. "That's right, sweetie."

As they were saying good-night, the sommelier hurried up, a bottle of wine cradled in his arms. With a flourish, he presented the French Burgundy to Noah. "For the lovebirds. We hope you'll find your stay on the *Empress* filled with romance. Ah, here's our photographer!"

The newcomer smiled in greeting. "How about a kiss for the camera?"

Keely blanched. "Oh, I don't think..."

"She's shy! Isn't that sweet?" Florence Hebert chirped.

The photographer hoisted his large professional camera. "This is on the house, folks, no charge. You'll want to show it to the grandkids someday."

"Go ahead, Keely," Beth teased. "We won't look."

Realizing it would seem unnatural for a honeymooning couple to refuse to share a kiss, Noah drew her into his arms. Tangling his fingers in her soft feathery hair, he tilted her head back, exposing her slightly parted lips, damp with... anticipation?

Then, incredibly, he forgot about the onlookers, losing himself in her dark eyes, smoky with an intensity he'd not noticed earlier; their depth hinted of secret pleasures. He sucked in a deep breath, startled by the dare so evident in the tilt of her chin.

Then his tongue touched hers and he was captive, even though he'd been the aggressor. He had no idea how long he remained her willing captive, but slowly, regretfully, he became aware of jovial hoots and catcalls directed at them.

Reluctantly releasing her sweetness, he drew away. "And *that* is why we don't have time for the casino," he said, wondering if Keely noticed the huskiness in his voice. Or if she, too, felt molten lava coursing through her veins.

WHEN THE OTHERS headed for the casino, Noah suggested he and Keely take a brief walk around the deck. "That's the kind of thing lovers would do on their first night at sea, isn't it?"

Still reeling from the kiss they'd shared, she didn't answer, but fell into step beside him. It was a glorious evening. The moon was full and pale, casting its golden shadow on the rippling water. Dinner had been tense, tiring. She'd never imagined how difficult it would be to maintain the charade. And when Noah kissed her...

No, she chided, her reaction had only been a release of the terrible tension. And now? a quirky inner voice prodded. What was her excuse now?

She knew it was the wine at dinner, the balmy sea air and the gentle splash of waves against the hull all working their magic on her. Yet as they sauntered in the peaceful quiet, she found herself drawing nearer to Noah, wanting to bask somehow in his strong maleness.

And he did look incredibly gorgeous tonight, she acknowledged. His creamy white dinner jacket and black tie lent him a James Bond elegance she found hard to deny. While the younger Noah had been cute and sexy, this older, more sophisticated version was breathtaking in his appeal.

She was going to have to watch herself, or... A shiver danced up her backbone and rippled along her shoulders at the thought of succumbing to her traitorous desires.

"What's the matter? Getting cold?" he asked.

Grasping at the pretext he'd offered, she nodded. "A little."

Noah stopped and peeled off his dinner jacket then draped it around her shoulders. "It's time to head back to the cabin, anyway. If anyone was watching us, we've either convinced them or not by now."

"Good idea. I'm exhausted."

A few moments later Noah slipped his card key into the lock and they entered the dimly lit stateroom. When they pulled aside the privacy curtain, it was immediately obvious that Manny had been in while they were gone. The wine was uncorked and breathing, a small plate of pastries was on the bedside table and the sofa had been transformed into a king-size bed. A bed that took up the entire living space.

A bed made for honeymooners.

They both stared for a long moment, then abruptly turned away and began rummaging in the built-in wardrobes for their nightclothes.

Casting about for a safe topic, Keely said, "I think dinner went pretty well, don't you?"

"I certainly enjoyed it—found it quite...stimulating. Think we convinced them?" Noah asked with exaggerated blandness, obviously referring to the kiss they shared in the dining room.

Quickly turning her head so he couldn't catch the telltale flush that heated her cheeks, Keely strove to keep her voice neutral as she changed the subject. "What did you think of our dinner companions?"

There was a long, tense pause. His voice suddenly as cold as the ocean depths beneath them, he said, "On the surface, they seemed like normal people on holiday. What was your take?"

She bit her lower lip and raised her fingers as she ticked off each couple. "The Greggs certainly seemed like your average Southern California yuppie couple. Nice, attractive—but possibly *too* normal?"

Noah leaned a hip against the television cabinet and nodded. "If I had set up this scenario, I'd want the contact to seem totally average so they'd fit in. Agreed. Beth and Steve are very possible. Next?"

"The Heberts." She laughed wryly. "First of all, I'm glad they're not my next-door neighbors. Can you imagine Willie and Florence popping in all the time to tell you about their darling son's difficult molar extractions?"

He chuckled at the thought. "What? You didn't find them scintillating dinner companions?"

"That's no reason to dismiss them as suspects, though," she said, yawning.

"Don't do that!" he demanded, then yawned widely himself. "Uh, you want the bathroom first?" Noah rubbed his palm against the dark stubble on his chin. The faint scratching sound tickled up her backbone like playful fingers.

"No, you go ahead." Keely moved away, dropping onto the edge of the bed.

He reached into a drawer and brandished an obviously new pair of candy-striped pajamas. "I want you to know I bought these for your benefit. I haven't worn pj's since I was ten."

She raised an eyebrow. "I appreciate the gesture."

"Don't you want to know what I usually wear?"

"Certainly not!"

He shrugged and flipped the pajama top over his shoulder as he sauntered into the miniscule bathroom and clanged the heavy metal door.

Keely slipped off her shoes and drew up her legs, wrapping her arms around her knees. Her overactive imagination had already conjured up an interesting alternative to his striped pj's. And she'd better just wipe that thought from her mind if she intended to get any sleep at all.

When he stepped out of the steamy bathroom a few moments later, his shirt was once again slung over his right shoulder. "I don't have to wear the top, do I? I'd suffocate."

She deliberately tore her gaze from his bare chest and washboard abs. "Wear whatever you like. Can I take my shower now?"

"Be my guest." He swept his hand low in a bowing motion. "Which side of the bed do you want?"

Mocking his largess, she bowed, as well. "Be my guest. Your choice." Grabbing the pair of thin sweats she'd brought for night wear, Keely made her escape.

When she came out of the bathroom, Noah was propped up on the right side of the bed, her favorite side, she noted. He was wearing a pair of aviator-style glasses and scanning a sheaf of papers. Funny, even the eyeglasses contributed to his rakish sophistication.

He looked up when she came into the room. "What about the Olstagens," he asked abruptly. "You never gave me your impression of Dieter and Maya."

"I don't know. Somehow I don't see a pair of Swiss nationals as our culprits. I certainly didn't notice an accent of any kind from whoever whispered to me at the lifeboat drill."

"What makes you so sure they're really Swiss? Dieter's accent was so thick it was almost a caricature."

She cocked her head, considering his theory. "That's certainly a possibility, but why are you leaning toward them as our culprits?"

He took off his glasses and gave her a long look. "Remember when we were all talking about our jobs and where we lived and so forth?"

"Yes."

"So where do the Olstagens live—what city? What do they do for a living?"

Keely thought for a moment. "I don't remember."

He sat up and pointed the arm of his glasses at her. "Do you know *why* you don't remember? Because they never told us, that's why."

"That's right!" She stepped forward and perched on the edge of the bed near his feet. "Every time the conversation turned to Maya and Dieter, one of them would change the subject."

He leaned against the padded headboard and slipped his glasses back on. "I say we put the Olstagens, or whoever they really are, at the head of our list. You pulled the sheet loose—cover my feet, will ya?"

Suddenly disconcerted by their intimate environment, Keely jumped off the bed and gingerly tucked the sheet around Noah's exposed feet. Trying to regain her equilibrium, she pulled her own reading glasses out of her handbag and dug out a novel she'd brought along. With great trepidation, she climbed into the other side of the bed. It was king-size and Noah was reclining almost on the far edge. Still, he was too close; she could smell his freshly showered body, clean and very male.

Opening her novel, she tried to concentrate on Dick Francis's latest racing mystery, but her eyes kept flickering to the man sprawled out beside her. After a moment she gave up and slammed the book closed.

He stacked his papers and glasses on the bedside table. "What's the matter, can't concentrate?"

"You're on my side," she groused.

"Too bad. You gave it away. Good night." He reached up and clicked off the small lamp above his head.

Turning off her own light, she nestled deep in the covers, certain his nearness would keep her awake all night. Surprisingly, Keely fell asleep almost immediately, as if lulled by his presence.

It was much later, when she felt herself being pulled toward wakefulness. Suddenly her eyes flew open and she was fully alert.

She stretched cautiously and stared unseeing into the inky darkness. She heard nothing and saw nothing, yet her heart was beating with the intensity of a snare drum and her mouth was dry and cottony.

Beside her, Noah was still, the warmth of his body caressing her flesh. But something was wrong.

It was then she heard the noise. A small, muffled sound, almost like an animal scuffling in the small vestibule by the door. Yet Keely knew instantly that no four-legged creature had invaded their privacy.

Someone was in their room.

Chapter Seven

Her heart in her throat, Keely started to slip from the bed when Noah's hand clamped around her waist. He hadn't been asleep, after all. Like her, he was lying still, waiting for the intruder to make the next move.

As her eyes adjusted to the dim filtered light, she could just make out the privacy curtain between the living area and the vestibule. The faint, furtive shuffling of feet told her the interloper was just beyond the curtain.

Again she started to sit upright, when Noah's strong hand on her shoulder eased her back down. He was telling her to lie still and keep quiet, but every fiber of her being screamed at her to jump up, yank back the curtain and expose the person who was skulking in the darkness.

Then, over the drumbeat of her heart, she heard the faintly metallic sound of the cabin door opening. A sliver of light peeked beneath the privacy curtain, then vanished as the door to their stateroom whispered closed.

The intruder was gone.

Noah sat up and placed a fingertip across her lips, gesturing for continued quiet. Then, moving with the silent, deliberate stealth of a prowling panther, he eased from the bed.

Keely felt rather than heard the soft pad of his bare feet rustling across the carpet. Her eyes, now accustomed to the near blackness, noted when he gently slipped behind the privacy curtain.

Anxiously she held her breath for a long, tense moment until again she heard the cabin door opening. There was a prolonged pause, then the door closed with a solid clank and Noah reappeared from behind the curtain. "Whoever it was is gone now," he whispered. "I don't think we should turn on any lights in case he's still out on deck."

Keely sat up in bed and tugged the thin cotton blanket beneath her chin. "What did he want?"

Noah flipped a small envelope onto the bed. "This note was just inside the vestibule. I heard something, then saw a shadowy figure pull back the curtain. The movement must have awakened you, because you stirred and our friend backed out of sight."

This undercover work was new, puzzling. Keely was comfortable and competent with straightforward crime investigation, but she felt out of her depth with all the cloak-and-dagger business.

She hated to expose her ignorance about the way the investigation was proceeding, but her cop's instincts kept telling her she was missing some piece of vital information. "Why? I mean, if he wanted to deliver a message, why wait until the middle of the night when we would surely be in bed? It doesn't make sense."

He cleared her purse and shawl off the small chair and carried it into the foyer. The chair legs scraped against the floor as he wedged it under the door handle.

"That should keep out everything but the bed-bugs," he whispered as he slid back into bed. "I don't think he'll be back, anyway. At least not while we're in the room."

Keely sank deeper beneath the covers until she felt the soft downy pillow cushion her neck. "Can we turn on the light yet? To read the note."

"Yeah. I guess it's okay now." He reached up and switched on the small overhead light. The envelope was part of the ship's stock stationery. Every room was furnished with a folder containing paper and envelopes. The note could have come from anyone on the ship.

Since there was no way to check the paper for fingerprints, Noah just ripped it open. A single sheet fluttered out.

He picked it up and read the block-print lettering aloud.

"Don't waste your time going ashore in Catalina. Stay on board and make new friends. We'll talk in Ensenada. Noon at Viva Zapata's Cantina. Don't be late. Come alone. Accidents happen to those who don't follow orders."

It was, of course, unsigned.

Noah yawned lazily. "Our friend's been watching too many B-movies. Actually, he could have just slipped the note under the door. I think the visit was two-fold. Get this message to us, but also let us know we're being watched. Of course, maybe he just wanted to see if we were really who we said we were."

"You mean if we were undercover cops, we most likely wouldn't be sleeping together?" The moment the words left her lips, she yearned to take them back.

Sure enough, Noah didn't let her poor choice of words pass without notice. "Ah, that's a perk I hadn't counted on. I like a woman who shows attention to detail. A woman who really involves herself in her work."

"Shut up, Noah."

"Gosh, I love marriage," he mumbled as he turned over and punched the pillow. "Try and get some sleep, Keely. Tomorrow could be a very long day."

No doubt, Keely thought. It had already been a very long night.

THE NEXT MORNING they had an uneventful breakfast by the pool. During the night, the *Empress* had anchored off the coast of Santa Catalina Island, a popular tourist resort twenty-six miles from the mainland, and accessible only by private plane or by sea.

Keely couldn't help but wonder at the crush of passengers gulping their breakfast in order to catch one of the launch boats to the island. Apparently the single day of shipboard leisure had already taken its toll on some travelers. Everyone rushed to line up for the shore excursion as though they were anxious to stand on terra firma once again.

Since the actual contact wasn't going to be made until they docked in Ensenada, Mexico, the next day, Keely and Noah had already decided to spend their day aboard the *Empress*.

They were quietly making plans to do a background check on some of their fellow passengers when a shadow fell across the table. "Good morning, love-birds!" Florence Hebert cooed. "Isn't it a lovely day?"

"Hi, Florence," Keely said between nibbles of a slice of papaya.

"Where's Willie this morning?" Noah asked as he drained his glass of freshly squeezed orange juice.

Florence rolled her eyes and picked at the pocket of her Hawaiian-print housedress. "Making reservations for a tee-off time. That man! We come all the way from Boise to see the exotic sites of California and Mexico, and he wants to spend his time on a golf course. Go figure. Are you kids coming ashore?"

Keely shook her head. The last thing she wanted was to spend her day shopping or sight-seeing with the gabby woman. Her time would be far better utilized helping Noah gather information.

After saying goodbye to Florence, they were heading through the lounge when they saw Steve and Beth playing pinochle with another couple. Noah grabbed Keely's hand and laced their fingers as they wandered up to the card players.

Her instinct was to snatch her hand away from the penetrating warmth of his, but Beth was watching them closely. Instead, Keely smiled and leaned against Noah, the way she imagined honeymooners behaved. His towering strength felt entirely too comfortable.

"Hey, guys," Steve said, being the first to look up. "Enjoying the cruise?"

Noah shrugged. "So far we've been too lazy to try any of the shipboard activities."

Steve patted his stomach. "I know what you mean about lazy. A few more seven-course meals and they'll have to roll me to shore."

Beth chuckled. "Listen to him—I had to literally pull him away from the midnight buffet last night."

Keely's instincts went on full alert. If the Greggs had been at the midnight buffet, then it was reasonable to assume they would have been up and wandering around an hour later—the same time someone was breaking into their room. Coincidence? Maybe...

She forced a casual smile. "If I was up that late, you wouldn't be able to drag me out of bed this early."

Steve shook his head. "For what this cruise cost, I don't intend to miss a single minute. Hey, I'm sorry, I should've introduced you to the Henleys." He pointed to their pinochle partners. "Dan and Mary Henley, these are two of our tablemates, Noah and Keely Bannister. Noah's the computer whiz I told you about."

Dan Henley was a large, bluff man in his early fifties. His rather bulbous nose was road-mapped with broken red lines. Although it was only shortly after nine, a Bloody Mary was at his elbow, an empty glass beside it. He folded his cards and peered at Noah through mirrored sunglasses. "Smart move, getting into computers these days. I'm in import-export myself. 'Course, no business can survive without computers."

"Dan, it's your play," Mary Henley said in an annoying whine.

Henley threw down a card and pulled the trick into his pile. "Say, Bannister, I'd like to pick your brain later. Want to ask you some questions about surfing the Internet."

"Don't know how much I can tell you," Noah answered. "I'm really into sales, running the store."

"Ah, that's great! You know, I'm working on a deal to import some software from Pakistan. Maybe we can talk."

"Sure, anytime. I'm interested in learning more about the import business myself." Noah tugged Keely's hand as if he were anxious to end the conversation.

She took his cue and smiled at the group. "We didn't mean to interrupt your card game. Maybe we can meet for drinks later this afternoon?"

"That'd be great!" Beth Gregg enthused. "How about the pool bar around five?"

"Sounds good," Noah said. "See you then."

As soon as they were out of earshot, Noah murmured, "Was it my imagination, or did Dan Henley seem overly interested in a relative stranger?"

"You mean that he struck up an acquaintance with the Greggs just to get to know us? That seems sort of convoluted." Even though they were no longer in sight of the cardplayers, Noah hadn't released her hand, and Keely was extremely aware of his touch.

Seemingly oblivious to her growing discomfort, he continued, "It was apparent they'd been talking about us. That has me wondering if the Greggs mentioned our names first, or if the Henleys led the conversation in that direction. By pumping the Greggs for information, Henley could keep tabs on us and we'd never know it."

Noah's argument made some sense. "Maybe he was just friendly. Mary gave me the creeps, though. I've never met such a cold fish."

"Yeah," he agreed. "They definitely are an odd couple. I think we should add them to our list of possible suspects. Speaking of which, I'm going up to the bridge to talk to the captain about using the ship-to-shore radio. It's already past noon in Washington, and

I want to get going on these background checks.
Where will you be?''

Keely froze and jerked her hand free. Obviously
Noah didn't intend to include her in this investigation
any more than he had to. She should have known he'd
try grandstanding on his own. Well, two could play his
game. She'd noticed Maya Olstagen heading into the
gym. This would be a good time to strike up a conversation with the Swiss woman.

Smiling innocently, Keely patted Noah's arm.
''That's a great idea.'' She hunched her shoulders and
rotated her neck. ''You know, I feel a little tense. I
haven't had a good workout since Rosie's—for a couple of weeks. I'm going to the gym, maybe sit in the
steam room afterward.''

His head bobbed in obvious relief that she wasn't
going to try to horn in on his investigation. ''After I
finish with the people in Washington, I'm going to see
if the captain will let me look at his passenger mani-
fest.''

''What will that tell you?''

''It'll tell me if the people we've met are using the
same names as on their passports.''

''Good plan.'' *What a waste of time,* she thought.
Why would the courier risk exposure by using an assumed name? At least it would keep Noah occupied
while she was busy with more germane inquiries.
Hoping to forestall any suspicion on his part, she
asked sweetly, ''Shall we meet for lunch?''

He glanced at his watch. ''Sure. The second seating
is at one. Let's meet in the cabin about half past twelve
so we can discuss anything I find out.''

Anything *he* finds out. There was no doubt he considered her a useless appendage. *Well, Mr. Noah Ban-*

Chapter Eight

After giving his assistant in Washington all the information he had on the passengers they'd met, Noah hung up the ship-to-shore telephone and turned to the *Empress*'s commanding officer. "Thanks for all your help, Captain. I especially appreciate your allowing me to receive messages on your private line."

The small man, resplendent in his gold-braided nautical uniform, accepted Noah's thanks with a nod. "Mr. Bannister, are you sure this...courier doesn't represent a danger to the passengers?"

While acknowledging Captain Jorgensen's concern, Noah readily assured him the courier would probably keep a very low profile. "He—or she—will be trying very hard to stay out of the limelight. I'm certain none of your other passengers will elicit any unwanted attention."

"I'll accept your professional judgment, Mr. Bannister, but I would ask that you keep me informed of any events that could affect my crew or passengers," he said, only a trace of his Scandinavian accent evident.

"I'll do that, sir."

"Good. When your people in Washington send back a reply, I will send one of my men for you. I shall put the message into your hand personally."

After once more thanking the captain for his co-operation, Noah glanced at his watch. It was almost twelve-thirty. He'd have to hurry if he was going to be on time for his luncheon date with Keely.

Keely.

Just thinking her name provoked musky reminders of her sweet scent in the bed beside him last night. So near and yet so far.

Thoroughly agitated now, Noah ignored the elevator and skipped down the three flights of winding stairs. Before his return to San Diego, he'd been completely over his infatuation with Keely Travers, had been for years—or so he thought.

Until the first time he saw her again. The damned woman must be some kind of enchantress. A witch.

His unflagging awareness of her sloe-eyed beauty and smoldering sexuality was bad enough. More worrisome was his fear that he might be losing his objectivity. Noah feared this investigation would prove Mike Travers was the informant, and that Rosie's guilt was indisputable. Why then, did he believe so strongly in Keely's integrity?

Because his judgment was being colored by his attraction to her, that's why. It was time to ignore his raging testosterone and pay attention to business. From now on, he vowed, he was going to keep a wide emotional distance from Keely. And as much physical distance as their cramped living quarters would allow.

Even as he made the commitment, Noah acknowledged how hard it would be to maintain.

Obviously relieved by her false playfulness, he countered, "Then we ought to get a move on, woman. Time's a wastin'."

Fifteen minutes later they slid into their seats at the table.

"Good morning, Keely!" their tablemates greeted her, almost in unison.

"How are you feeling, hon?" Florence Hebert reached over and patted Keely's hand.

"Much better. Thank you."

Steve Gregg shook his head as if truly perplexed. "We heard about your accident. They said you got stuck in a steam booth?"

"That's right," Keely said, draping her napkin across her lap.

"That's so weird. But I once got locked in my own bathroom," Beth confided. "I told Steve the lock was sticking, but did he fix it? No, of course not."

"I did so," Steve protested.

"Sure. After I was stuck in there for over an hour."

While the Greggs bickered and Fernando poured coffee, Keely glanced across the table at Maya Olstagen. While everyone else had expressed their concern for Keely's well-being, Maya hadn't uttered a word.

She looked up now and caught Keely's thoughtful gaze. "Your face is still red," Maya blurted, "otherwise you look fine."

"No thanks to the prankster who locked the door."

"Oh, come on, Keely. You don't think the door was intentionally jammed, do you?" Willie Hebert was clearly skeptical.

Noah stirred his coffee and took a sip. "Since a steel bar was wedged between the door handle and the jamb, I'd say that was a pretty good sign she was deliberately locked in.''

A stunned silence clouded the atmosphere. Dieter finally broke the hushed chill. ''*Ach du lieber!* Thank goodness you were found in time. For that, we must be grateful.''

As Fernando served their fruit cups, Florence cast a murderous scowl at her spouse. ''At least your husband came looking for you. I think if I was missing less than a week, Willie wouldn't even notice I was gone.''

''Now, Flo, you know that's not true. Besides, they're newlyweds. Course he missed her.''

As if suddenly reminded of his role, Noah wrapped a protective arm around her shoulders. Still stinging from his rebuff in their room, Keely smiled sweetly and shrugged off his hand.

While the busboy picked up their empty goblets, Fernando returned with their breakfast. Keely had ordered French toast, and the thick, fragrant chunks of sweet Mexican bread captured her full attention. Served with slices of mango and papaya, the combination was exactly what her empty stomach needed.

She was cutting into her second slice when Maya addressed her. ''Keely, do you have any idea who it was? The person who locked you up like that?''

''I don't have the slightest notion, Maya. But you had only been gone a moment. Are you sure you didn't see anyone?''

The blond woman cocked her head and stared into space as if mentally retracing her steps that day. ''No. I don't think so. I'm certain the corridor was empty when I left the gym. Although the Greggs were in the card room.''

Beth Gregg looked up sharply. "We were playing pinochle. What's your point?"

"Oh, no slur intended," Maya said quickly. "Just pointing out to Keely that I wasn't the only person in the vicinity."

Dieter patted his wife's hand. "Darling, don't excite yourself. I'm sure Keely wasn't accusing you of anything."

"I'm not so sure." Maya arched a fine, golden eyebrow. "Were you accusing me of locking you in, Keely?"

BY THE TIME they headed down the gangplank, Noah couldn't wait to get off the ship. He hated petty bickering, and Maya's defensive attitude had almost turned breakfast into a brawl.

From Keely's stiff shoulders and thrust-out chin, he could tell she was still fuming over the way Maya had upset everyone.

One moment, Keely had been stealthily interrogating the Swiss woman, the next moment, Maya was practically accusing Keely of fabricating the entire episode.

Tempers had flared and the Olstagens had ultimately left the table in a huff. Noah couldn't decide if Maya's indignation was indicative of her guilt or her innocence. If she was the person who had bolted the steam-room door, would she want to call attention to herself by flagrantly sparking a verbal battle?

On the other hand, if she was innocent, what was she so steamed about?

At any rate, Maya Olstagen was the least of their worries right now. They had nearly two hours to kill before their assignation at Viva Zapata's Cantina, so they decided to do a little sight-seeing.

Keely's hopes for a cool day were dashed by soaring temperatures. The thermometer was already approaching the ninety-degree mark. And it was barely ten in the morning.

Still, they had both dressed for the heat. And as Noah strolled behind Keely, he was truly grateful for the heat wave. Her gently swaying hips, clad in close-fitting white shorts, held far more interest for him than any trinket the street vendors were trying to hawk.

Even though they'd eaten scarcely an hour before, Keely insisted they stop at a roadside stand for a fish taco. Although the local specialty sounded a bit exotic for Noah's tastes, he was pleasantly surprised when he bit into the messy treat.

After they'd used up his supply of paper napkins, the taco vendor happily directed them to a nearby open-air market. As they made their way between the crowded stalls, Noah watched Keely's eyes light up when she saw other tourists loudly bargaining for rock-bottom prices.

He could tell she was anxious to join the fray.

Keely had already bought a colorful serape blanket, a huge straw handbag and a gaudy piñata in the shape of a parrot when Noah decided to get her out of the market before they had to rent another stateroom just to store her bounty.

Slinging the serape over his shoulder, he took her elbow and led her firmly toward the exit. "I hate to come between you and your bargains, but we need to find that tavern."

Keely pointed to a passing booth. "Wait, wait! Did you see those onyx candlesticks? They were magnificent!"

"Yes they were," he agreed calmly. "So was that chess set and those lace tablecloths. But we have an appointment, remember?"

She glumly fell into step beside him. "I know, but...something in me would just like to forget about this whole mess. Just enjoy the holiday like everyone else."

"Yeah, but we've got a job to do."

"Even if everything goes according to plan and we take possession of the plates, it's still like sticking our pinkies into a dike. Stopping one engraver isn't going to keep the bogus money out of circulation."

He shook his head. "Quit talking like a fatalist. Cops can't afford to think that way and you know it. We'll stop this counterfeiter today and another crook tomorrow."

She flung out an arm, indicating the exotic locale surrounding them. "Just look at this beauty, Noah. People like us are never able to appreciate beauty. We keep plodding through the slime looking for more slime."

He whistled for a taxi and hustled her inside. When the door shut and he told the driver their destination, he leaned back against the tattered leather seat. "So you never have time to smell the roses? Why don't you give it up, move to Mexico and spend your days sipping margaritas and dancing with mariachis?"

Sullen silence was her only response.

Noah not only understood, he identified with her mood. He, too, got fed up with arresting sleazeballs who were usually out on bail before he finished the paperwork. But the job was its own reward in a way.

She didn't move to Mexico or Barbados for the same reasons he didn't. A cop was a cop, and there was nothing they could do to change their way of thinking. Besides, running away to an idyllic life would only be idyllic if there was someone to share it with.

The cab turned onto a side street near the center of town, and immediately a loud, raucous cacophony filled the air. The driver pulled over in front of a run-down-looking bar, which was the obvious source of the blaring music and hoots of laughter filtering outside.

"Lively little bistro," Noah commented.

"Mmm," she agreed. "With so much commotion going on, it's the perfect place for a clandestine meeting. Unless one of us dances naked on the tabletop, I doubt anyone will notice us."

He glanced at her slender legs peeking out of her white shorts. "If either of us has to dance naked, you have my vote."

"Here you are, señor, Viva Zapata's Cantina. A very famous place."

Noah paid the driver and added a generous tip. He stuffed the Mexican blanket into Keely's new straw bag, but there was no room for the ridiculous paper parrot. Rolling his eyes, he tucked the bag and the bird under his arm and they headed for the door.

Standing outside the saloon-style doors, Noah suddenly regretted having left his revolver on board. He'd made the decision for two reasons: first, of course, was the well-known antipathy of the Mexican authorities for foreigners who brought firearms into their country; second, he thought it probable that the courier might frisk him before completing the transaction. It would be dicey explaining why the husband of a gambling housewife would be carrying.

Now, those reasons felt like weak substitutes for the security of his gun.

Still, it was the middle of the day. The streets were teeming with tourists and locals, and if the sound level was any indication, Zapata's was packed. He was being overly cautious, probably because Keely was along and they were in a foreign country. Everything would be fine.

His hand was on the swinging door when Keely screamed.

Chapter Ten

"My purse!" Keely shouted as she tore past him. "That man grabbed my purse."

Momentarily stunned, her words finally registered and Noah raced after her. A half block away he glimpsed a young boy darting between startled onlookers, Keely's black leather purse dangling from his hand.

"Stop, thief!" she shouted as she ran in pursuit. The thief didn't stop, nor did any of the swarm of people attempt to hinder his getaway.

"Keely, wait up!" Noah called over the street noise, but if she heard him she ignored his directive.

At any other time, Noah thought, he would have overtaken her in a few strides. But with her straw bag smacking his thighs with each step and the damned parrot obstructing his vision with its molting paper feathers, it was all he could do to keep her in sight.

In the distance, he saw the purse snatcher disappear around a corner. By the time Noah reached the intersection, Keely was waiting, doubled over and hands on her knees, her breath heaving.

"Wh-where is he?" Noah puffed up beside her.

She shook her head. "I think he went into one of these stores, but I didn't see which one."

Plucking a purple "feather" out of his mouth, Noah handed her the scraggly bird and straw bag. "Go back to Zapata's and wait for me while I check out a few of these storefronts."

Keely's backbone visibly stiffened. "I'm not a wilting female you have to coddle. I'm perfectly capable of helping you conduct a search."

"Oh, good, Keely. Let's stand here and play games while the thief gets away with your credit cards, money and passport. Did you forget we were supposed to meet someone at Zapata's in—" he pointed to his watch, "—exactly three minutes?"

To her credit, she didn't argue further, but simply nodded and started trotting back toward the cantina.

"Don't leave Zapata's for any reason before I return," Noah called to her retreating back.

He watched Keely till she disappeared around the corner, then he glanced over the small crowd still huddled around him. The knowledge that Keely was preparing to meet the courier alone prodded him with a sense of urgency.

Fighting a growing sense of impending trouble, Noah ducked into the first shop.

BY THE TIME Keely made it back to Viva Zapata's, she was overheated and winded. The unaccustomed lack of physical activity over the past few days, combined with her ordeal in the steam booth, had taken a toll on her stamina. She leaned against the dingy adobe building to catch her breath and swipe her hair back into place before she went inside.

Feeling a moment's apprehension because she had no idea who or what would be waiting for her, Keely took a deep breath and pushed open the swinging saloon doors. The noise level in the dim, smoke-filled bar was almost overwhelming.

As she stepped into the murky interior, she was startled when a shadowy figure materialized behind her. "Señora Bannister?" he asked in a husky, mildly accented Latino voice.

"Yes." She started to turn around when he jerked her shoulders.

"Don't look back. I have a delivery for you. It is better for everyone if you don't see me. Now, keep your eyes in front, *sí?* Now walk toward the ladies' facility to the left of the bar."

It was going down, and she was all alone. Keely did as she was told, starting at the bold catcalls and whistles that followed her progress.

"Do not pay attention to those men. No one will harm you," the unseen man behind her said. "Continue walking, señora."

It wasn't the rowdies at the bar who worried her. It was the cold, indifferent tone of the courier's voice, as if it made no difference to him whether he delivered the package or slipped a switchblade into her back.

"Are you Roberto?" she asked.

"If that is who you want me to be, *chica*."

She stopped. "I was supposed to meet Roberto here."

He nudged her sharply. "I'm the man you were supposed to meet. Keep moving."

To distract herself and to look for possible allies should she need help, she glanced at her fellow patrons as she slowly tramped past. The men who took

soon, the *Empress* would be getting under way without them.

In an effort to speed the proceedings, Noah had told the captain he was a U.S. government official and that his identification was in his wallet. Rather than speed up the process, this information slowed their interrogation to a snail's pace.

The Mexican police captain jumped to the immediate conclusion they were in his country on an undercover operation for the CIA. Noah had denied the charge time and again, to no avail.

Suarez stood up and beckoned his assistant to follow him. They stood in the far corner and conferred in mumbled Spanish, casting occasional glances first at Noah, then a long, studied gaze at Keely.

As if aware of their scrutiny, she dropped her gaze to the large straw purse in her lap. Without loosening her death hold on the handle, she let it slide over the edge of the chair to dangle out of sight. Noah knew if they subjected her to even a cursory search, they would surely find those engraving plates and all hell would break loose.

He didn't relish the notion of being subjected to hours of questioning—south-of-the-border style. And the thought of Keely at their mercy was more than he could bear.

Hoping to distract them, he called out, "Say, Captain, can we get this show on the road? Our ship will be sailing soon, and I'd hate to miss it."

Suarez swaggered back to his desk and clutched his hand to his chest in mock distress. "Señor, does this mean you are not enjoying our hospitality?"

"More than I can say." Noah smiled agreeably. "But the little woman has been a bit under the weather lately and—"

Once again Captain Suarez spoke in rapid-fire Spanish to Jorge, who translated. "He says he will talk to your wife in a moment. First he wants to know why you are doing American police business in his city and did not pay him the courtesy of checking in with his office?"

Noah ran his fingers through his already-jumbled hair and exhaled, a long sigh of frustration. "No, no, no. We've been over this at least a dozen times. Mrs. Bannister and I are on a holiday—not police business. We were sight-seeing when that kid grabbed her purse."

Jorge repeated his answer to Captain Suarez, who turned and gave Keely a sharp glance. "Why didn't you stay with your husband, instead of going to a notorious bar?" he asked through the translator.

This was the first time the police official had directed his questioning to Keely. Noah held his breath, wondering how she was going to respond. While he had done a fair amount of undercover work during the course of his career, this was Keely's first covert assignment. She hadn't had time to refine the fine art of subterfuge.

Giving Noah a stricken glance, her fingers tightened around the handle of the straw bag, as evidenced by her white knuckles. Clearing her voice, she asked for a glass of water—an obvious stalling tactic.

Suarez glanced at the straw bag but seemed reassured by the silly parrot piñata peeking out the top. He cocked his head and studied Keely's white face. "*¿Esta enferma?*"

Noah understood Captain Suarez's question. He wanted to know if Keely was ill.

The captain poured her a glass of water from a bottle on the corner of his desk and crossed the room to hand it to her, concern creasing his forehead.

"No, I'm not really sick," she murmured. "I'm just a little...queasy." She patted her stomach for emphasis and suddenly Noah understood. She *was* feeling ill. Once when he'd gotten into trouble at school, Keely had taken up for him by telling the teacher a huge whopper. A moment later she'd rushed out of the classroom and thrown up.

Keely couldn't lie. Her conscience resided firmly in her stomach and refused to allow any untruths. It was up to him to think of a good story to cover her actions.

It was on the tip of his tongue to say something about Keely going to the bar to phone for the police when Captain Suarez clapped his palm against his forehead. *"¡Ah, comprendo!"*

He patted Keely's shoulder, then swiftly crossed the room and pumped Noah's hand. Noah didn't know what the man thought he understood, but it had certainly changed his attitude. Instead of eyeing them with unconcealed suspicion, his brown eyes glowed with good humor as he chattered and laughed.

Completely at sea as to how he should react to this startling transformation, Noah turned to Jorge. "What's he saying?"

To his amazement, the young officer blushed furiously, his complexion turning a dark siena. Lowering his gaze, he mumbled, "He is offering his congratulations."

Noah glanced at Keely. She looked as bemused as he felt. "Congratulations?"

Again Jorge blushed. "For your baby, señor. Isn't your wife feeling sick because she is getting a baby?"

As comprehension dawned, a broad smile lit up Noah's face. Captain Suarez had given them the perfect out. He thought Keely had returned to the bar because she was suffering from morning sickness.

Accepting the captain's congratulations, Noah stood up and walked to her side. Wrapping a protective arm around her shoulder, he said to Jorge, "Tell the Captain we appreciate his concern. But if there's nothing else, perhaps I could take the little woman back onto the ship now?"

While Jorge translated his request, Noah smiled down at Keely. Her eyes glittered dangerously but she didn't say a word.

Captain Suarez eyed his "guests" for a long time. Finally he nodded. He spoke at length and Jorge snapped to attention and translated. "Captain Suarez wishes to extend his apologies for any inconvenience you have suffered. He hopes that one day you will return to our fair city, where you will of course be his guest. A car will take you back to the wharf."

Relief washing through him, Noah stood up and made an elaborate pretense of helping Keely to her feet. "Please tell Captain Suarez I appreciate his personal attention. Can I have my watch and wallet now? We really need to get back to the ship."

"Of course."

After several effusive goodbye handshakes, Jorge wandered down the hall. He returned a moment later with Noah's belongings.

Jorge pointed to the doorway. "Come. A car is outside."

They thanked him for his help as he ushered them to the waiting squad car. The late-afternoon sun was slanting across the dusty, cobbled street and the evening smells of fried onions and fresh tortillas wafted in the air, reminding Noah it had been a very long time since breakfast.

When they slid into the back seat, he reached into his pocket for the newly returned watch. Jorge directed the driver to take them to the dock, then offered a farewell salute. They waved back and settled in the seat while the car glided into traffic.

"Whew," Noah said. "I was beginning to think we'd never get out of there."

Keely slowly twisted around until her deep brown eyes were burning into his. "'The little woman'?" she remarked. "You called me the little woman?"

Noah snapped the band around his wrist and leaned back against the seat, closing his eyes. This was obviously not the right time to give her more bad news.

It was well past five and no doubt the *Empress* had long since set sail without them.

They were stranded in Mexico.

Chapter Eleven

Not only was the *Empress* gone from her moorings, she had left the harbor and completely disappeared from sight. They couldn't even hire a launch to take them out to meet the liner. They were well and truly deserted in Ensenada.

Keely stared at the vast empty space where the ship should have been anchored. "It's gone!"

Without opening his eyes, Noah said nonchalantly, "I thought it might be."

"What do we do now," she asked, "sleep on the beach and hitchhike back to the States?"

He sat up and rubbed his eyes. "Why, my dear wife, I thought you'd be more inventive than that."

Keely crossed her arms and plumped back against the car seat. "Listen, *husband,* you got us into this mess—waving your badge at Captain Suarez—so it's your turn to be inventive."

Noah chuckled at the absurdity of it all. What a hell of a day this had turned out to be. "First, we'll find a hotel. We'll have dinner, get some sleep and tomorrow make our way back to San Diego by land. We have three full days to get back to Long Beach. Piece of cake."

Keely continued to glare. "Yeah, and if I know you it'll be *devil's* food cake." She held her handbag aloft. "At least we have money and credit cards, no thanks to your ill-advised orders."

Determined not to let her sour observations spoil his sudden, unaccountably lighthearted mood, he said jauntily, "Good! Then dinner's on you. Take us to a nice hotel in town, amigo," he told the driver.

When they walked up to register at the La Posada del Sol, the clerk gave no overt notice of their rumpled appearance and lack of luggage. Since Ensenada was only about 90 miles from San Diego by land, apparently lovers' trysts were not uncommon occurrences in the local hotels. In order to save their cash for emergencies, Keely put their room bill on her credit card.

"Do you have a hotel safe?" she asked as she signed the transaction slip.

The clerk smiled, showing a row of even, incredibly white teeth. "But of course. You have valuables you wish to check?"

She turned to Noah and spoke softly. "What do you think?"

He considered the idea. "We have to shop for a change of clothes and toiletries, then eat dinner somewhere. I don't want to leave it in the room. In fact, after all the trouble we've been through, I really don't want to let the package out of my sight."

Keely nodded in agreement. "Still, we have to eat dinner someplace. If we carry this thing everyplace we go, someone's apt to think we're carrying drugs or something."

"That's true. I guess the safe's . . . safe."

Keely withdrew the parcel and handed it to the clerk. After obtaining a receipt, she asked about dinner.

"Oh, we have the finest restaurant in Baja," the clerk said with obvious pride. "And tonight is our weekly floor show. Folkloric dancers and mariachis. You won't want to miss it."

"Sounds great," Keely said. And it did. A night of complete hedonistic pleasure was exactly what she needed. She wanted to be a tourist, eat rich food, drink one too many margaritas and dance in the street. Mostly she wanted to forget she was only in the idyllic setting with Noah because of their mutual business.

"What time?" Noah asked. "Should we make reservations?"

The clerk nodded. "I can do that for you, sir. Around seven?"

When they nodded, he scribbled on a slip of paper and handed Noah a room key. "Number fourteen, second floor. But there is one thing..."

"Oh, forgive me." Noah reached into his pocket for a bill. It had been so long since he'd visited Mexico he'd completely forgotten that tipping was de rigueur for almost every service.

The clerk expertly palmed the money. "Thank you, sir. But I was going to say that... er, shorts are not allowed in the dining room after five. But we have a fine clothing shop right here on the premises."

He pointed out a corridor leading to the hotel's shopping facilities and they followed his directions to a large, brightly lit *tienda* with a surprisingly broad selection.

After making several purchases, Noah carried their bounty up to their room. When he opened the door, they were both startled by the sumptuous decor. Spacious and bright, the room had an uncarpeted tile floor, and a filmy white spread covered the king-size bed. The windows were undraped, but their privacy was guaranteed by diaphanous white sheers.

The room was understated and elegant.

Keely dropped her almost-bald paper parrot onto the bed with their other parcels and strolled into the bathroom. A moment later Noah heard her squeal and went rushing in behind her.

"What's wrong?"

She was standing in the middle of the room, her back to the doorway, arms spread wide. "Look at this bathroom!"

He glanced around. Looked like a bathroom to him. "What about it?"

She whirled to face him. "Have you no soul? Look at this place—it's fabulous."

He leaned against the doorframe and crossed his arms. "I'm not really into plumbing fixtures as long as they work."

She pointed to the huge sunken tub in the corner. "A person could hold an orgy in that tub."

"Ah. Now you have my interest. Is that an invitation?"

Her extended arm swung around until she was pointing behind him at the doorway. "Get out of here, peasant, and leave me to my bath."

He unfolded and started out of the room, pausing in the doorway. "That's such a big tub, it seems a shame to waste all the water it'll take to fill it. I'm heavily into environmental concerns, you know."

"Oh, you are?"

"Uh-huh. Mexico has a real water shortage here in Baja. It would promote good international relations if we helped them conserve water, you know."

"I see." She nodded slowly. "And you propose to help out Mexico—in fact, help out the world—by sharing a bath with me? To conserve water, of course."

"Seems like a fine idea to me."

Moving like a lightning bolt, she reached around and yanked a towel off the rack. Holding one end behind her back, she snapped the towel like a whip, stinging his thigh.

"Ouch!"

"That's the lousiest excuse for a pass I've ever heard."

"You told me to be inventive," he complained, rubbing the red mark on his thigh.

"Now I'm telling you to get out," she said, holding the towel poised.

"As long as you're sure I can't help you wash your back or something?"

"Out!" But a telltale blush crept up her cheeks and Noah was convinced she found the idea as intriguing as he did.

He found himself whistling as he dropped onto the bed for a quick nap before they had to dress for dinner.

"KEELY, HURRY UP in there! It's almost seven."

"For heaven's sake, Noah, chill out," she called from behind the bathroom door. "This is Mexico—nothing happens on time, including dinner."

She put a fresh layer of pink gloss on her lips and patted her hair. Not bad, she reflected, considering she'd had to make do without a blow dryer or curling iron, both having been left on board the *Empress*. Finally satisfied, she picked up the lacy shawl she'd purchased in the gift shop and went into the bedroom, where Noah was pacing a path in the terra-cotta tile.

He stopped abruptly as she appeared in the doorway. A vaguely husky quality in his voice, he said, "You look...fabulous."

"You like it?" Keely asked tentatively. She had felt self-conscious donning the white embroidered skirt and matching shoulder-baring ruffled blouse. Her legs were bare and she wore a new pair of leather huaraches that squeaked slightly when she walked. With her ink-black hair, Keely knew she could pass for a local woman, and the appreciative stare on Noah's face told her the unaccustomed attire was flattering.

"You don't look so bad yourself," she said, casting her own favorable glance at Noah. He was wearing white peasant trousers and an aqua shirt with full sleeves that reminded her of something a pirate might have worn a couple centuries ago. All he needed was an eye patch and that stupid parrot piñata on his shoulder.

Her stomach grumbled suddenly, reminding her of another, more immediate appetite that still needed satisfying. "Ready to go?"

"I've been ready for twenty minutes," he grumbled, locking the door behind them.

When they walked down the broad stairway fashioned from colorful Talavera tiles, Keely stopped short.

"What's wrong?"

Edging closer so she wouldn't be overheard, she murmured, "Look over there by the waterfall in the lobby."

Noah scanned the area and shook his head. "What about it?"

"Don't you see them?"

"Who?"

Lifting her hand ever so slightly, Keely pointed surreptitiously. "There, almost hidden by the potted palm next to the waterfall."

His gaze followed her fingertip. A middle-aged couple was sitting side by side on a bench near the waterfall, not talking, simply watching people stroll past. Flo and Willie Hebert should have been sailing south toward Mazatlán, not sitting in the lobby of the La Posada del Sol.

Noah took Keely's elbow and they slowly continued descending the staircase. "I don't like this," he said.

"Neither do I," she muttered back between clenched teeth as they crossed the lobby and approached the lounging couple.

"Look who's here, Willie—the Bannisters!" Florence jumped heavily to her feet and smoothed her blue-and-white floral housedress.

He stood up to join his wife. "What're you folks doing here? Though I must say we're mighty glad to see you."

He pumped Noah's hand with so much enthusiasm, Keely found herself marveling at the depths of their obvious relief. She smiled a greeting. "We lost track of time. What happened to you guys?"

Willie nodded and wiped a plump white hand over his balding pate. "Shopping, that's what happened. We missed the danged boat! This woman—"

"Now, hon, these people don't want to hear our marital squabbles. Say, we were just fixing to go into dinner. Care to join us?"

Keely shot Noah a glance and he raised his eyebrows as if to say, *What else can we do?* He signaled to the headwaiter and changed their dinner reservation to four. A moment later they followed him to a balmy patio overlooking the indigo ocean below. Flickering torches were staked among potted plants, offering the only lighting besides the luminous moon.

"My stars, what a view," Florence said as she peered over the stone railing.

The waiter passed around menus, but after a quick glance, the Heberts deferred to Keely and Noah. "You folks are from around these parts, so you order," Willie directed as he slammed shut his menu.

Florence closed hers, as well. She leaned across the table and whispered loudly, "You don't suppose they use any kind of...domestic animal in their food, do you?"

Keely noted Noah rolling his eyes before he ducked back behind the menu. "No, I'm sure not," she reassured the older woman, before hiding a smile behind her own menu.

When she'd sufficiently recovered enough to speak, Keely said, "Noah, go ahead and order for all of us. I'm so hungry I could eat a whale if you pulled him into shore."

The waiter appeared and Noah ordered avocado-and-shrimp salads and sole Veracruz for everyone. As they plunged into the chips and salsa while waiting for their salads, Keely tried to find common ground with the older couple.

"Do you have just the one son?" she asked.

"Oh, yes. Hank's just the apple of our eye, he is that."

Noah broke a tortilla chip with a loud snap. "Hank? I thought the other night you told us your son's name was Tommy."

There was a sudden, foreboding silence before Florence said, "Why, Noah Bannister, what a good memory you have. Of course you're correct. You see, we named him after both our fathers— Thomas Henry Hebert. So sometimes we call him Tommy, but sometimes he's Hank or even Henry."

Although Flo Hebert's explanation was quick and facile, Keely still held a few misgivings. So did Noah, judging from the guarded expression on his face and the thinly veiled questions he continued to ask during their dinner.

Could the Heberts be their shipboard contacts? Was it possible that Flo had been the person who locked her in the steam room? Keely's nerve endings twitched as she considered the possibility of that seemingly vacuous face hiding a dark, menacing personality.

Still, even if the Heberts had been sent to keep an eye on them, what could they do now? The plates had already been transferred and were secured in the hotel safe. Except for a few minor problems, their plan was exactly on schedule. As Noah would say, *No problema.*

Satisfied that she could forget about the plates, at least for the evening, Keely savored the tangy rice that accompanied the fish.

After dinner, while serving a relaxing cup of Kahlúa coffee topped with whipped cream, the waiter suggested they adjourn inside because the floor show would soon begin. He led them to a tiny table only a few feet from the stage, where they had front-row seats for the colorful pageant.

As more and more people crowded into the room, their chairs were jostled closer and closer together until Keely found herself sitting thigh to thigh with Noah. She tried to concentrate on the fiery Mexican dancers who were doing a very seductive flamenco, but her concentration kept drifting to the warm pressure against her thigh.

The temperature in the room started to rise as the excitement level of the dancers reached a fevered pitch. The woman's red satin skirt flashed as she was wooed by the male dancer. Then their roles switched and she became the pursuer, her dark eyes half-closed and enticing.

Noah's hand closed over hers. She glanced at him; his full attention was on the flamenco dancers, but his thumb rubbed its own sensuous path on her skin.

On stage, the tempo increased. Faster and even faster until they whirled in a breathtaking display of color and pure sexuality. Keely swiped a hand across her forehead. It was so hot in the room. Her pulse was pounding, almost in time with the chattering footfalls of the dancers.

Then Noah's fingers moved over her own and her breath caught in her throat. Suddenly, Keely understood. The only rising heat in the room was being produced by her own body. Assisted, of course, by Noah Bannister's unconscious gesture.

She breathed in relief when the provocative dance ended in a blaze of blue lights and flashing feet.

Then a marimba combo took the stage and encouraged the audience to try their own dancing skills on the postage-stamp dance floor. When the leader asked for requests, Keely was mortified by Willie Hebert jumping to his feet and announcing the Bannisters were celebrating their wedding and "How about a real slow dance for the lovers?"

The band was only too happy to comply. Since there seemed to be no alternative, Keely and Noah rose to their feet to a smattering of applause. A blinding spotlight followed them onto the deserted dance floor.

As the combo broke into a hauntingly sensuous version of "Besame Mucho," Noah hauled her into a close embrace. The past ten years faded into oblivion as she snuggled into arms that had once held her through a hundred dances. The slightly off-key singer crooned about needing many kisses from his lover and Keely could suddenly identify with that need.

It had been so long since she'd given herself to the music—and to the man holding her. He pulled her tighter, until she could feel his hot breath on her neck, the brush of his lips caressing the tender area behind her ear. She felt like a candle left in the hot sunlight— she was melting fast.

As the music changed tempo, she barely noticed, so transported was she into another time, a softer, gentler place.

A world that held only the two of them. A time she wanted to last forever.

The dreamy mood was interrupted when Willie Hebert cut in. Holding her stiffly at arm's length, he said,

"You two dance like you've been together for years instead of a few weeks."

"Mmm." She smiled noncommittally. "How about you and Florence, do you go dancing a lot?"

He shook his head. "Nah, she's not much of a party animal, I'm afraid. So how did you say you and Noah happened to miss the boat—ship, I mean?"

Recalling the Heberts own excuse for becoming stranded south of the border, she said, "Florence and I seem to have a lot in common. I was shopping, too."

"Is that a fact?" But there was a sudden, subtle shift in his tone. The buffoonish tourist had disappeared, replaced by a far more thoughtful inquisitor.

Keely was greatly relieved when the dance ended and Noah reclaimed her.

As if the party mood had deflated, no one returned to the dance floor. They sat at the tiny table a while longer, indulging in desultory conversation, but clearly something had happened to alter the chemistry between the two couples.

Finally, Flo yawned. "I don't know about you kids, but I've had about enough fun for one evening. What say, hubby, ready for bed?"

Willie drained his beer and hoisted himself out of his chair. Giving Noah an exaggerated wink, he snickered, "Hey, when you've been married as long as we have and the little woman still can't wait to get you in the sack, must be doing something right, huh?"

Noah smiled weakly and lifted his hand in a farewell gesture. As they made their way out of the patio bar back into the main lobby, he turned to Keely and grinned. "Whew! A little bit of Willie-boy goes a long way, doesn't it?"

She smiled ruefully. "Besides being a bit of a chauvinist piglet, there's something rather disconcerting about him. I mean, he plays the backwoods buffoon so well I keep expecting him to show up in baggy overalls and chewing on a piece of hay!"

"I know what you mean." Noah nodded thoughtfully and stared into the lobby, where the Heberts could still be seen in front of the elevators. "It feels like an act. As if Willie's acting out the stereotype of a Midwestern rube."

"Do you think he's involved in this?"

He shrugged and rose to his feet. "Let's say he sure bears watching. Enough about Willie Hebert. How about a moonlit stroll on the beach?"

"Sounds heavenly," she murmured. In fact, walking on a moon-drenched beach with Noah was the best idea she'd heard in a very long time.

Noah dropped a handful of pesos on the bright plaid tablecloth and draped his arm around Keely's waist, leading her to a side door that led directly outside. The stiff breeze coming off the ocean had picked up in intensity. Without the sun's warming rays, the air was brisk to the point of chilling.

On their way to the beachfront, they looped along the wooden sidewalk beneath their bedroom window. Keely paused as a gust of wind whipped around the corner. Although Noah's body served like a protective windbreak and blocked most of the breeze, Keely drew a sharp breath at the sudden coolness on her flushed skin. She shivered and wrapped her arms around herself.

"You're cold!" Noah exclaimed, drawing her closer. "Maybe we should just go back inside."

"Oh no!" she protested, a bit too enthusiastically. "I'll be fine, really. A good brisk walk will warm me right up." She hated to admit, even to herself, how much she was looking forward to a little quality time with Noah, without pretense or a scripted agenda to follow. Maybe they could even recover some of the good times they'd shared long ago.

Noah stopped and looked back at the hotel. "I wasn't exactly thinking of a speed walk, you know. I had something more...leisurely in mind. Why don't I run upstairs and grab your shawl?"

"Oh, no, that's too much trouble. I'll be fine."

But he'd already released her waist and was trotting toward the side entrance. "Won't take a couple of minutes. Enjoy the moonlight until I get back."

While she waited Keely leaned against the sturdy trunk of a towering palm tree. Beneath her thin cotton blouse she could still feel the warm imprint of Noah's hand against her waist. Earlier she'd been disturbed by the way her body had betrayed her during the flamenco performance, when she'd been too aware of Noah's presence for comfort.

Even now, with Noah out of reach and out of sight, she couldn't rid her mind of him. Each moment he was away from her seemed endless, she acknowledged, glancing up toward their second-floor window. The understanding of how much she had come to count on his presence was startling. And terribly disconcerting. For ten years Keely had trained herself to rely on no man, to keep her own counsel and let no one slip beneath her defensive shell. Yet, somehow, Noah had managed to do just that. Again.

Now, for instance, he'd only run up two flights of stairs to retrieve her shawl, but to her overwrought senses it seemed he'd been gone entirely too long. She glanced up at their window, expecting to see the light flash on; instead, what she saw was both confusing and unnerving.

Initially Keely mistook the pinpoint of brightness for a flickering shadow cast by the moonlight. But as she watched its stealthy pattern sweep the expanse of their hotel room, she quickly realized someone was covertly searching with the aid of a flashlight. It wasn't Noah; he hadn't enough time to reach the room yet. Besides, he would have simply turned on the overhead light.

What would happen if he walked in and caught the intruder off guard?

She opened her mouth to shout a warning but realized that to do so would also alert whoever was in their room. She could do nothing to help, unless . . . Keely turned and ran toward the door that Noah had so recently entered, hoping to catch him before he burst in on their unwelcome guest.

She'd only gone a few feet, however, when she heard a commotion from above. The unmistakable sounds of furniture being knocked over, of men shouting and then . . .

A loud, reverberating gunshot echoed in the night.

Chapter Twelve

Walking down the empty corridor toward their hotel room, Noah found himself whistling a jaunty tune. He didn't have to wonder why. He was truly enjoying his evening with Keely, and looking forward to what else the night might offer. Thanks to the magical Mexican moon, the strain between them had mercifully faded into oblivion, at least for one night. But that was enough right now. Tomorrow could take care of itself.

Tonight he was grateful for the opportunity to explore the possibility of what might have been. If he and Keely hadn't been such adolescent fools so long ago.

Pausing at the door for his room key, Noah's thoughts were lingering with the lovely woman waiting below, so it was without second thought that he unlocked the door and stepped inside.

He turned to reach for the light switch when he was hit from behind with tremendous force.

He staggered forward, falling onto his face beside the bed. His head was ringing from the blow and his eyes hadn't yet adjusted to the darkness, but Noah sensed another imminent attack. Rolling left, he slipped under the bed just as something bright and heavy flashed past his eyes and thudded on the bare tile floor.

Instinctively reaching out, Noah snagged the weapon the intruder had dropped. He'd hoped for a gun but was grateful for the comforting heft of the stainless-steel flashlight.

Sliding farther under the massive bed, Noah slipped out the other side and stood to face his attacker. He was still woozy from the blow to his head, but he managed to hold tight to his makeshift weapon while he concentrated, trying to regain his equilibrium. He was able to discern a faint movement on the other side of the bed as the intruder took a stealthy step toward him.

Noah raised the flashlight over his head and poised on the balls of his feet. When the shadowy figure inched within striking distance, Noah swung with all his might.

A heavy moan followed by an ugly curse told him his swing had solidly connected.

The figure stumbled backward, falling against the dresser. The ceramic vase filled with fresh wildflowers hit the tile floor with a crash. Seizing the momentary advantage, Noah leapt forward, swinging the flashlight in a wide arc in front of him. The steel batonlike weapon swished through the air, but the attacker had backed out of range.

"Come on, you bastard," Noah gritted between clenched teeth. "Why don't you come out and fight like a man?"

The stranger's heavy breath as he panted with exertion was the only response, until a flash of moonlight filtering through the open window exposed his silhouette. He was holding a gun.

Grabbing the wooden chair from the dressing table, Noah pitched it with all his might into the interloper's chest.

The air sucked out of the man's lungs with a ferocious whoosh and Noah followed up by ramming his head into his stomach. But the determined burglar didn't release his hold on the gun.

Noah hadn't trained for years in hand-to-hand combat to be repelled by the aggressiveness of his opponent. Locking both his hands around the hand holding the gun, Noah dragged him across the room until they crashed into the dresser. The man struck Noah's wrist with the gun butt, and the piercing pain caused him to drop his only protection. The flashlight rattled across the tile floor before disappearing beneath the bed.

Lunging after it, he held on to his opponent's wrist as they careened into the bedside table, knocking it over with a loud whack.

In that moment Noah realized the sounds of their furious battle could be heard in the courtyard below. Keely was bound to hear the noise and come running upstairs. Right into the firing line.

Fear for her safety gave Noah the physical strength to challenge Goliath. With a roar of unadulterated fury, he threw the shadowy figure to the floor.

But the intruder held on to the gun, and in the murky moonlight Noah saw the barrel swivel toward him. He ducked just as a loud explosion pierced his eardrums, then a dark gouge appeared in the white plaster near his head.

Before he could move, the gun barked again.

Dropping to the floor, Noah rolled and crawled across the room until he could see the line of light from beneath the bedroom door. Five more feet. If only he could get to his feet, open the door and run for safety—before the assassin nailed him.

The would-be killer had lost sight of him in the darkness, Noah realized, as the man's footfalls padded across the room toward him. He stepped on the throw rug two feet away and paused, listening for any telltale sounds that would betray Noah's whereabouts. Noah held his breath. Only a protective shadow from the immense wardrobe hid his body and kept the man from spotting him and shooting him at point-blank range.

Using the dregs of his energy, Noah's fingertips inched to the edge of the throw rug and he yanked with all his might, knocking the assailant off his feet. Growling with fury, he smashed the gunman's head against the tile floor.

What he wouldn't give for his own revolver right now! The man had fallen onto his gun and Noah couldn't reach it. His only hope was to run and get Keely to safety before the man recovered from the repeated blows he'd taken.

Rolling away from the stunned man, Noah stumbled toward the door, tripping over Keely's straw bag, which had been knocked into the middle of the floor during the melee. Remembering why he'd come upstairs in the first place, to fetch Keely's shawl from the straw bag, Noah bent over and searched for the elusive bag.

By now the intruder was rising groggily to his feet. Noah knew he had only a few more seconds.

If it wasn't for Keely, he'd stay and somehow beat the truth out of their night visitor, then turn the creep over to the police. But Noah was unsure about the sanctity of certain members of the Ensenada police. Was it mere chance those officers had happened upon him while he was chasing the purse snatcher? Was it simply politics that kept them detained in Captain Suarez's office until long after the *Empress* had set sail?

Since he was certain a payoff had been made to someone in the San Diego PD, how could he assume that the Mexican police hadn't been bribed, as well?

He couldn't risk it, not with Keely's life at stake.

Noah's scrambling fingers at last found the familiar feel of the straw handle.

The man was now on his feet and struggling to raise his gun hand. Frantic, Noah searched for something to use as a weapon, but only a couple of bed pillows were in reach. Snatching the white bedspread, he tossed it over the assailant's head like a net.

With any luck the maneuver would give him a few precious seconds to make his escape. Noah dodged into the hall and ran for the back stairs. Even as he rounded the corner, he could hear footsteps pounding up the steps.

Someone had heard the scuffle—hotel security or the assailant's partner? He had no way of knowing so he simply ran back down the rear stairs.

He skidded to a halt on the landing, realizing someone was running up the stairs toward him. Noah hunkered down in preparation for tackling the second opponent, when Keely's slight form came into view.

Her face was a white mask in the darkness. Wordlessly, Noah grabbed her hand and pulled her down the narrow staircase behind him. Like the true professional she was, she sensed and accepted his urgency without question. Her grip was firm and her breathing was even. Noah couldn't believe how well she was maintaining her cool.

When they reached the bottom level, they heard the sound of heavy footsteps coming toward them.

"Quick!" Keely whispered. "This way."

She pointed to a side door all but hidden by a maid's cleaning cart parked in the dim hallway.

They slipped out the door and emerged in the courtyard they'd seen beneath their bedroom window. Trapped! He knew if they tried to make it across the open courtyard, they'd be exposed to anyone following them through the side door, not to mention the gunman in their bedroom. Their best chance was to hide and try to bluff the killer into believing they were gone.

Sliding along the shadowy surface of the building, they ducked down behind a large Dumpster and waited. With a few tersely whispered words, Noah explained about the gunman waiting in their room.

A shadow fell over the arched doorway leading to the courtyard. His heart beating a primal rhythm in his chest, Noah maneuvered between Keely and the doorway. If the gunman burst into the courtyard, Noah only hoped he could distract him long enough for Keely to make an escape.

To his immense surprise, no one followed them.

"Are you all right?" he whispered.

"Yes," she answered, her breath pumping in short, furious bursts. She huddled against him and wrapped

her arms around herself as scant protection against the
cool night breeze. "Why did you stop to get my bag?
He could have killed you!"

"Shh," Noah cautioned. Keeping one eye on the
door, he reached into the straw bag and pulled out
Keely's shawl. "Here. Wrap this around yourself and
let's get out of here."

"What about the box in the hotel safe?"

Damn! He'd forgotten about the engraving plates.
Well, they'd just have to come back for them later.
Right now he wanted to get Keely far away from this
hotel before they fell prey to a second assault.

"We can pick up the plates tomorrow when the
lobby's full of people. I don't think he'd try anything
in front of a dozen witnesses."

"Good point," she whispered as she wrapped the
lacy shawl over her chilled upper arms. "Besides, why
cause suspicion by having the manager open the safe
in the middle of the night?"

Noah glanced at her. "You ready for some serious
jogging? Our friend could show up any second."

"Then what are we waiting for?" she asked as she
darted away from the sheltering Dumpster and ran,
light-footed, toward the street.

Surprised by her abrupt movement, Noah quickly
recovered and trotted after her. As they ran silently
through the courtyard, he recalled how quickly Keely
had adjusted to their dangerous situation and sprung
into action. The woman was a miracle—adaptable,
resourceful and damnably sexy.

It was almost a shame the pain of their past would
rob them of a future.

Right now, however, he had to concentrate. If he didn't stay alert, there was every chance their future wouldn't extend to dawn.

With no planned destination except away from the hotel, they negotiated the dark, deserted streets of Ensenada. Up one alley and down another. They wound along the hillside, hitting dead ends, climbing fences, always heading for the edge of town.

Endlessly. Blindly. Until they were thoroughly lost and utterly haggard. Never once did Keely complain or ask for a breather. His estimation of her professionalism rose with each moment and each obstacle they had to overcome. She was one hell of a cop.

Finally, too exhausted to stumble another foot, they came to a clearing just outside town. Apparently they had found a farm, because the main house was ringed by a half-dozen ramshackle outbuildings. Moonlight filtering through the clouds exposed endless fields in the distance, and the air was heavy with the smell of newly plowed earth.

Keely and Noah were so fatigued, they scarcely noted the wonder of their surroundings.

Acting more on instinct than strategy, they staggered toward the barn. Inside, the air was redolent with clean hay and the warm musky scent of animals. As they padded through the darkness, a cow lowed and a horse neighed briefly, then all was still again.

They found an empty stall and Noah pitched a mound of fresh hay. In moments they flopped onto their primitive bed and huddled together for warmth.

She nestled against his warm body, reveling in his solid masculine hardness. He'd only given her a sketchy outline of what had transpired in their hotel room, but Keely knew without asking that he'd opted to flee instead of fight because of her. He'd chosen to let his case fall apart rather than expose her to danger. When was the last time a man had chosen her well-being over his own ego?

She smiled in the darkness, whispered good-night and turned on her side, not trusting herself to breathe in his familiar scent.

But she couldn't fall asleep, she was too full of adrenaline and memories.

In the darkness, Noah's hand rustled through the fragrant straw, seeking hers. Every self-preserving instinct was screaming for her to move away, to put emotional if not actual distance between them.

Suddenly his whisper filled the night air. "You're not asleep, either, are you?"

"No," Her voice was a squeak.

"I've tried not to notice, you know."

"Notice what?" she breathed.

"The way your skin glimmers like satin in the moonlight. The way you always smell fresh. That tiny little spot behind your ear that's demanding to be kissed."

The straw shifted as he moved closer. He was so near she could smell the scent of soap on his skin, and her imagination pictured him taking her here and now.

Keely knew how close she'd come to losing Noah tonight. She shuddered as she recalled the horrifying reports of the gunshots, sounds that chilled her soul. She'd been so afraid, so completely terrified that she'd lost Noah—again.

Her years of pent-up resentment and hurt had melted beneath her fear. Even now, when every protective instinct shouted for her to hold on to the hate she'd been nurturing for so long, the emotions flourishing in her breast urged her to let go.

Pain and bitterness were now...yearning and exhilaration. It was both scary and exciting.

In many ways Noah Bannister was annoying—too macho and stubborn. But it felt very...right having him in her bed—even if her bed was only a simple straw pallet.

It was as if she'd unconsciously been waiting a very long time for him to return and complete the dance they'd begun ten years before.

Dreamlike, she moved over just a little, until her hand found the warm, vital flesh just above his rib cage.

He groaned and reached for her. Suddenly, Keely was in Noah's arms and the last ten years disappeared as quickly as her white peasant blouse.

During their ill-fated teenage romance, they had shared more than one frenzied, frustrated petting session in the back seat of Noah's beat-up Plymouth Duster. Noah the boy had been as unsure as she was and their untried passion had never led them to its natural, ultimate conclusion.

But this was no boy with her now, and Keely knew this seductive, vital man would not be denied. As if in a trance, she watched as his fingers rose to her face, caressing her cheek, then trailed slowly, tantalizingly down her throat.

"I was so frightened something would happen to you," he said sliding his hand to the back of her neck, burrowing in her short, dark tresses. "I couldn't stand to lose you. Not again." With a deep groan, he drew her mouth to his. Keely sighed with wanton abandon as her own traitorous body reached eagerly for his.

His lips were lush, sensual. Incredibly soft against
hers. Noah encircled her in his arms and began kissing her more deeply. Each thrust of his tongue se-
duced her, teased her with provocative seeking. Keely's
breath lurched in her chest. Her senses reeled crazily,
out of control, until she was mesmerized by the sweet
taste of his lips.

She slid her arms up his back, pulling him close until her breasts were crushed against his chest. Her nip-
ples prodded the soft mat of dark hair on his chest.

She wanted their kiss to last for eternity, to hold
them captive in this perfect moment, but her body had
a will of its own, wanting, insisting, demanding.

Like a wildfire burning out of control, the embers
ignited by his kiss spread throughout her body until
she was singed by the hard heat that proclaimed his
arousal to be as strong as her own.

Yes, she wanted to go on kissing him, to go on
drowning in the intimacy of his touch. But Keely knew
that, finally, she needed more. Much more.

Cupping her face in his hands, he whispered
breathlessly in the darkness, "God, how I've needed
you. For so long. So very long." His mouth de-
scended on hers again, and her heart cried out with
joy. He needed her. Wanted her. As she'd yearned for
him all of these empty, wasted years.

He turned away from her briefly, and in the ambi-
ent moonlight sneaking through a slat in the plank
wall, she saw him slip a silvery foil packet from his
wallet. Noah had always watched out for her, and it
warmed her to see that even now, in the white-hot
flame of their desire, he was still protecting her.

As he turned back to envelope her in his embrace,
her senses were heightened beyond belief. She could

feel the whisper of his beard lightly grazing her skin as he kissed his way down her stomach, and back up her legs. Her insides were liquid and she felt like a caldron of need, about to boil over.

As if sensing the urgency of her desire, Noah rose above her and lowered into her, and she cried out with the fulfillment of a promise too long in the keeping.

How long, how very long she'd wanted, needed this man. How foolish she'd been ever to believe she'd be free of the sweetly torturous hold he had on her.

And, for once, she didn't care about tomorrow.

Giving herself completely to the moment, Keely refused to dwell on the consequences—she just wanted this one night of love.

Even if Noah was only extracting payment for a decade-old debt.

LATER, A LONG TIME LATER, she turned in his arms and inhaled the fragrantly combined scents of fresh hay, night-blooming jasmine and Noah's own intoxicating maleness.

"Do you think it was Willie Hebert who attacked you?" she whispered in the darkness.

Noah pulled her head onto his shoulder and murmured into her hair. "I'm almost certain of it. Tomorrow morning I intend to have a very thorough discussion with our erstwhile shipmates."

Keely stifled a yawn and nestled contentedly into the crook of his neck. "Are you sure that's a good idea? Maybe we should just head north so we don't miss the contact at Long Beach Harbor."

"We'll make it. But a talk with Hebert is overdue."

From the steely resolve in his voice, Keely knew Noah had more on his mind than simple conversation. She also had no doubt the pudgy salesman was going to come up short in his *discussion* with Noah.

As fatigue and spent passion finally overtook them and they succumbed to sleep, Keely had a fleeting thought that Noah Bannister was probably the best cop she'd ever worked with. Quietly competent, determined and fiercely loyal. He was also an incredible lover. Truly incredible.

THE SUN was already high in the sky when Keely's eyes fluttered open. For a moment she was disoriented, finding herself naked in a pile of straw, covered only by the inadequate protection of her shawl.

Then she remembered.

She smiled and turned toward Noah, but only the indentation where he had lain in the warm, fragrant hay was there to greet her. Puzzled, Keely sat up and looked around.

A strange man was blocking the doorway to the stall.

And he had a pitchfork aimed at her heart.

Chapter Thirteen

Instinctively, Keely clutched the shawl to her breast and stared with breathless terror at the Mexican man wielding the pitchfork.

For a long, anxious moment they faced one another until the man lowered the pitchfork and fired off a stream of Spanish.

Noah was the one who spoke and understood the language. Where in blue blazes was he? The ugly thought crossed her mind that Noah might have abandoned her to go after Willie Hebert. If that was the case, she was going to wring his neck—unless this man dispatched her with his pitchfork first.

Now that the first heart-wrenching moment of fear had passed, Keely was virtually certain he meant her no harm. Dressed in the unbleached cotton trousers and loose shirt of a farmer, he was no doubt as startled by her as she was by him.

And his face, seamed by too much time in the sun, hinted that his age might be well over seventy. He was simply an old, frightened farmer, probably unaccustomed to finding naked women in his barn.

Keeping that thought firmly entrenched in her consciousness, she smiled up at him. *"Hola, señor."*

Gesturing toward her, he again rattled off a stream of Spanish words. Shrugging carefully lest she dislodge the scant protection of her shawl, Keely dredged up a phrase of high school Spanish and mumbled, *"No hablo español."*

She finally understood that he was questioning her about her lack of attire. She pointed to a jumble of clothes in the corner and waved her hand, somehow relating to him that she'd get dressed if he would turn his back.

"Bah!" The old man snorted and turned away long enough for her to scramble into her clothes. When she timidly stepped toward him, he beckoned her to follow him.

She blinked as they stepped out into the hot sunlight, just in time to see Noah sauntering into the clearing, a broad grin on his face. He had both hands full of red, juicy-looking berries of some kind. The farmer raised his pitchfork and Noah's smile faded.

Slowly, one step at a time, Noah advanced toward them, keeping his eye firmly focused on the farmer and his pitchfork. *"Buenos días,"* he said, smiling widely at the farmer. *"¿Cóma está?"*

The old man hitched his thumb at Keely. *"¿Su esposa?"* Your wife?

Noah nodded and launched into a long, halting explanation in what even Keely knew to be badly fractured Spanish. Still, he must have convinced the farmer because the old man slowly lowered his pitchfork and listened intently. After a few moments he asked, *"¿Tiene hambre?"*

Noah turned to Keely. "This is Señor Dorado and he wants to know if you're hungry."

"Famished," she said, suddenly realizing just how hungry she was.

Noah relayed her answer to Señor Dorado, who waved toward his humble farmhouse. They followed his lead into the one-room adobe structure. Although tiny and simply furnished, Mr. Dorado's home was clean and well ordered. The farmer, obviously proud of his home, sat them at the table and offered coffee.

In the corner, a short, well-rounded woman of about the same age was sautéing something that smelled wonderful. She wiped her hands on a stained apron and bustled over to the table, nattering at her husband the whole time. With a welcoming smile, she patted Keely on the cheek and nodded pleasantly to Noah.

In minutes, Señora Dorado delivered a luscious meal of fresh flour tortillas and eggs scrambled with onions, peppers and chilies. The plates were garnished with the sweet berries Noah had picked and given to the woman.

When the older couple joined them at the battered wooden table, Keely heartily ate the simple meal, unable to remember the last time anything had tasted so delicious.

In the past twelve hours, *all* her appetites had been whetted. And sated.

After they pushed away from the table, their stomachs stuffed beyond belief, Keely offered help with the washup but Mrs. Dorado refused with effusive thanks. Her husband also declined any payment for their meal, then offered to take them back to Ensenada in his pickup.

"Only if you'll let me reimburse you for your time and gasoline," Noah insisted in broken Spanish.

He and Señor Dorado haggled for a few moments before the farmer gave in with a grin, and they knew the wily old man had outnegotiated them.

After bidding his wife farewell, they piled into the rickety truck and headed back toward town.

In moments they were off the unpaved roads and jostling along the cobbled streets of Ensenada. When Mr. Dorado pulled to a halt in front of their hotel, Keely couldn't believe how fast the trip had been. Last night they'd wandered for what seemed hours; while this morning their return had taken only a matter of minutes.

Despite vehement protests from Mr. Dorado, Noah handed the elderly man twice the sum they'd negotiated for and led Keely back into the lobby.

Taking her elbow, Noah led her to the shelter of a towering palm tree while he scanned the open area. No sign of either Hebert.

They cautiously approached the desk and asked if there had been any messages. The clerk checked the box and shook his head. "No, señor. Will you be staying another day?"

Nothing in his demeanor gave any indication that the police had responded to a disturbance in their room the night before. "No, please prepare our bill," Noah said. "We'll be checking out shortly."

"Very good, sir."

"So far, so good," Noah breathed in her ear. "Let's just act as if nothing's happened and hope for the best."

"Suits me," she whispered back. "But the sooner we get back over the border, the happier I'll be."

Their ascent to the second-floor room was uneventful and they paused outside the door. Extracting his room key, Noah stepped inside first. Except for the utter disarray, nothing seemed to be missing.

Keely stepped into the room behind him and stared around her in wide-eyed wonder. "That must have been a heck of a fight last night."

Noah grinned, looking for the world like the boy who'd taken on and bested the neighborhood bully. "You oughta see the other guy," he said as he began setting the furnishings back on their feet.

Keely picked up the white spread off the floor and started toward the king-size bed. She stopped suddenly and gasped aloud.

Noah was picking up shards of the ceramic vase when he heard Keely's loud drawn-in breath. He turned, took in her stunned expression and quickly moved past her to look behind the bed.

A man was lying on the floor, his head and upper torso hidden by a jumble of bed sheets. His legs curved outward at improbable angles. He was dreadfully still. Not a muscle twitched. Noah took a heavy brass lamp from the bureau and held it high, just in case. But he didn't think he'd need the weapon.

When he saw the deep red smear trailing down the man's dark blue shirt and onto his tan trousers, Noah was certain. Still, he motioned Keely to stay back and eased along the bed frame until he was beside the body. He hunkered down and placed his fingertips on the cold, motionless neck. No pulse.

Noah pulled aside the bloodied bed sheet that had been carelessly draped over the top half of the body. The slack face of Willie Hebert stared back with unseeing blue eyes.

The front of Willie's powder blue shirt had been stained a deep, solid crimson. He'd been shot in the back, as evidenced by the gaping exit wound in the front of his chest. Poor Willie had met his maker several hours before. There was nothing they could do for him now.

Taking care not to contaminate the crime scene, Noah backed away. Keely was standing behind him. He took her elbow and led her away from the grisly scene. "You don't need to see this, Keely. Come on, let's get out of here."

She jerked free. "You seem to keep forgetting I'm a police officer, Noah. This isn't my first dead body, you know."

But he saw the high points of color on her cheeks. Keely was one of those unfortunate cops—good at her job but far too gentle to ever become sufficiently hardened against the violence.

Giving her time to regain her composure, Noah began searching the room for anything they might have left behind. There was nothing of importance, and he knew they had to get out of there—pronto. As soon as the maid arrived and found the body, all hell was going to break loose.

As if picking up on his thoughts, Keely said, "We'd better get that package. We need to get as far away from here as possible before the police arrive."

"Yeah. I think Captain Suarez might not take it so kindly if we show up back at his jail, accused of murder."

Finding the Do Not Disturb sign on the floor, he slipped it over the doorknob on their way out. Maybe they could buy a little more time.

Keeping her voice hushed as they walked toward the stairs, Keely said, "What about Florence?"

"Or whatever her real name is."

"What do you think has happened to her?"

He cupped her elbow as they started descending the broad tile staircase. "She might be waiting around to see if we show up, but I doubt it. My guess is that she's hightailing it out of town before her so-called husband is found."

Keely gasped. "You think she did it?"

"She's certainly a prime suspect. Otherwise, why hasn't she raised a ruckus about her dear spouse missing all night? Since we're supposedly the only people she knows in the city, wouldn't she have come to us for help?"

"But why? What possible motive could she have for shooting her husband? Someone else could be on the trail of those plates," Keely insisted. "Who wants them bad enough to kill?"

Lowering his voice even more as they approached the registration desk, Noah nodded to the clerk, who was on the telephone. "I'd bet a month's pay that old Flo's our killer," he said. "Who else could it be?"

Maybe one other suspect, Keely thought, as a painful shaft of suspicion sliced through her.

There was one other person who knew about the plates, who knew Willie Hebert was in their hotel room, who possibly had access to Willie's gun last night. Noah was alone with Willie Hebert for several long minutes during the course of their altercation. She'd accepted his version of the facts without question. But...what if things hadn't gone the way Noah had described them? What if he'd overpowered Willie Hebert and killed him with his own gun?

Noah was always to quick to place the blame on someone else—Rosie, her father, someone in the San

Diego PD. What if all his accusations were deliberate efforts to direct suspicion away from himself?

Why hadn't Willie Hebert put more effort into pursuing them when they'd fled the hotel last night? Maybe because Willie was already dead.

No, it just couldn't be—not Noah. She was letting her imagination run away. Still, she'd already remarked on how different Noah was from the boy she remembered. Did she really know this man enough to trust him with her life?

The clerk hung up the phone and came over to help them. Noah settled their bill and handed him the claim check. They waited anxiously while he went into the back office to retrieve their package.

Noah drummed his fingers on the tile countertop while Keely's mind beat out a horrifying rhythm of its own. Could Noah really have killed Willie Hebert? How could she even think it?

She didn't want to accept the possibility of his guilt, especially not after the way he'd held her last night. But all the strange happenings of the past few days were starting to mount up.

And everything was connected to Noah Bannister.

After she signed for the package, they stepped away from the counter. Pausing near the cooling waterfall, she said hesitantly, "You know, I feel funny about running away and leaving Willie's death unreported. I've been a police officer too long, I guess."

He snorted. "You're not a cop here. If Suarez finds out we've been involved in the murder of another tourist, we could spend the rest of our lives in a Mexican jail."

"Oh, come on, Noah. You're a cop—sort of. If Suarez finds out that we went into that room and didn't report the body, we'll never convince him of our innocence."

They stepped out of the cool lobby into the dazzling, hot sunlight. Noah turned to face her. "You do what you like. I'm not getting involved with the local authorities until I have these plates safely back across the border."

"Ah, yes, the precious plates!" she snapped. "I'd forgotten that nothing else in life is important to you except those plates."

He whistled for a taxi and stared at her blankly. "What's gotten into you this morning? You know perfectly well these plates are why we came to Mexico in the first place. Of course they're important to me."

A battered cab pulled up to the curb beside them and Noah opened the rear door. When they settled gingerly onto the hot vinyl seat, he faced her and added sharply, "Since we have every reason to believe Rosie's death was connected to those plates, I'd think nailing this counterfeit gang would be equally important to you."

Turning away from the brutal honesty of his words, she pushed down the ugly thought roiling in her subconscious and said, "So what do we do now?"

"Head for the border."

AN HOUR LATER, a typical young Mexican couple from the country stepped off the city bus at the central station and approached the ticket window. The man was wearing the dusty white garments and faded straw hat of a farmer. The woman with him wore a dark maroon shawl draped over her head and shoulders and carried a heavily packed straw bag.

A beleaguered-looking piñata peeking out of the bag was the only note of incongruity.

They'd talked about taking the bus directly to Tijuana, the sprawling industrial city across the border from San Diego. Noah had argued that Willie's killer would be watching the border crossings, but he would also be looking for a couple, so they decided to go part of the distance, then spend the night in a hotel, and in the morning they'd split up and make their way north to Tijuana and across to San Diego. Without a weapon or any way to obtain one, it was the only plan they felt had a chance of working.

They inched up to the ticket counter and Noah pulled the brim of his battered hat lower over his face. He slid a handful of pesos under the steel grid and mumbled, *"Dos para Rosarito."* Rosarito Beach was a small tourist town only a scant twenty miles from the California border.

The clerk took no particular note of the pair. He slid two tickets under the grid with a sprinkling of coins. Then he fired off a stream of Spanish and pointed at a rickety-looking bus a few yards away.

"Gracias." Noah pocketed the change and held the tickets in his hand.

As soon as they were out of earshot of the vendor, Noah whispered in Keely's ear, "So far so good. I think he said that's our bus over there."

"I hope so." Keely tugged on his sleeve and bobbed her head toward the station. "Looks like we have company."

Two khaki-uniformed policemen, fully armed with assault rifles, were slowly walking along the sidewalk in front of the station. They seemed to be scanning the crowd carefully, as if they were on the lookout for someone in particular. Perhaps a pair of Americans who had fled the scene of a murder? Keely thought with a shudder of apprehension.

Picking up their pace slightly, Noah and Keely followed a straggly line moving toward the bus. A man in a blue uniform, too tight for his ample belly, was collecting tickets.

Out of the corner of her eye Keely saw the policemen heading their way. She prodded Noah in the side, and he nodded to show that he, too, had seen the men approaching.

Only a half-dozen people were left between them and the bus. "Come on, hurry!" Keely urged under her breath. But the slow-moving farmers continued their snail's pace.

Finally they were next.

Noah handed their tickets to the heavy man in the blue uniform. He tore them in half and handed the stubs back. He stared at them for a long, breathless moment. *"¡Pasale!"* he growled, waving a hand up the steps.

She didn't need to be bilingual to understand he was telling them to board.

They had just settled in on a ratty bench seat near the rear of the bus when the policemen boarded. The men slowly made their way down the center aisle, gazing intently at each occupant. In a few seconds they would reach Keely and Noah.

What could they do to deflect attention?

If they'd been in the States, Keely would have kissed Noah or argued with him. But she knew public displays of affection were frowned upon below the border and, with the bare minimum of Spanish words in her vocabulary, she couldn't make an argument look convincing.

Noah had leaned back in the seat and flipped his straw hat over his face as if sleeping. But the ruse apparently wasn't going to work. One of the policemen nudged the other and nodded at Noah.

She had to do *something*.

Suddenly she recalled a single word she'd learned from a Latina girlfriend in high school. There was a dance and one of the boys had spiked the punch. Keely's friend, Delia, was furious with her boyfriend because he'd imbibed too much punch and was staggering on the dance floor.

Remembering Delia's embarrassed epithet, Keely wound her shawl tighter across her face, doubled her fist and socked Noah on the arm.

"Ow!"

Flapping the straw bag in front of his face, she chastised, *"¡Borracho!"* the Spanish word for drunkard. Turning away from him as if in a tiff, she glared out the window.

The two policemen laughed aloud, heckled Noah good-naturedly and left the bus.

IT SEEMED as if they'd stopped at every wide patch in the road, Keely reflected as she wearily climbed off the bus late that afternoon. The driver had taken the access road instead of the new highway, and they'd jostled over potholes and ruts for mile after rugged mile. After their scare at the station in Ensenada, however, there had been no further brushes with the authorities.

Keely was bone weary and wanted nothing more than a cool soothing drink and to flop into bed.

The bus dropped them off in front of the Rosarito Beach Hotel, a lovely old dowager slightly past her prime. Still, the bright murals decorating the walls and the paddle fans whooshing above the lobby spoke of the genteel elegance of a time gone by.

Before they'd left the bus, Keely had given Noah half of the money she was carrying, because they'd decided not to use their credit cards unless absolutely necessary. By using cash they could check in under an assumed name. In honor of the kind farmer who'd taken them in, they presented themselves to the desk clerk as Mr. and Mrs. Dorado.

While Noah had their parcel placed in the hotel safe, Keely wandered into the gift shop just off the lobby.

She strolled the aisles, admiring the Mexican handicrafts, papier-mâché birds on gilded swings, gaudy crepe-paper flowers, gaily painted pots and a multitude of onyx chess sets.

Finally choosing one of the large chess sets because it came in a box similar in size to the one that held the engraving plates, she carried it to the front counter and asked that it be wrapped in plain brown paper.

The clerk offered a bright floral gift wrap, but she shook her head firmly. "No. Brown paper," she pointed to the clerk's camel-colored shirt.

He shrugged and pulled an empty grocery bag out from behind the counter. *"¿Bien?"*

"Yes, that'll do just fine."

By the time he finished wrapping the parcel, Noah was waiting by the elevators. Silently they rode up to the next floor.

Their room was in the rear of the hotel, overlooking the Olympic-size pool and with a far off view of the Pacific Ocean, ringed by royal palms. The scene was both energizing and idyllic, but the charms of the sleepy little town were wasted on Keely.

Upstairs, Noah gave the room a cursory security check, then wrapped an arm around Keely's sagging shoulders. "I'm going downstairs and scout around. Make sure Florence Hebert isn't lurking in the lobby. Why don't you take a nap, then I'll try to catch one when I get back. Until we're safely across the border, I think we should take turns staying on guard."

"Mmm. Good idea. I hope there's a tub and not just a shower. I want to soak for at least an hour."

He laughed. "I bet a change of clothes would feel pretty good. I'll see what I can rustle up."

"You're a saint, Noah Bannister."

He cupped her face in both hands and dropped a kiss onto her forehead. "You're pretty incredible yourself, Keely Travers. Now go lock yourself in the bathroom before I change my mind and join you."

He started out the door and paused. "I'll take the key in case you're sleeping when I get back." For an endless moment he stared into her eyes, his own filled with an unfathomable softness.

"See you in a bit," he whispered and closed the door behind him.

AFTER HIS FOOTSTEPS faded down the hallway, she headed for the bathroom and once again was delighted by the sumptuous fixtures. If there was one thing that Mexican builders did well, in Keely's opinion, it was bathrooms.

A huge sunken tub took up an entire corner of the spacious room. A tub she intended to soak in for the next hour. She turned the spigot and a stream of clean, hot water splashed into the tiled bathtub.

She stripped off the clothes that bore little resemblance to the fresh white ensemble she'd first donned yesterday. Grabbing a tiny container of shampoo and conditioner from a straw basket on the vanity, she eased into the steaming water.

Oh, heaven, she mused as she sank back, enjoying the cool tile behind her neck and the hot water swallowing her shoulders.

But her overwrought mind wouldn't allow her to relax totally. They had the plates, that was the good news. But Keely felt more uncertain, more confused than ever. Although he was careful not to say so, she knew Noah still believed her father was involved in the counterfeiting operation. And even though her body still trembled at the memory of Noah's caresses last night, she still harbored a few doubts about him.

The only certain thing was that the Heberts hadn't been operating alone. Someone had leaked their true identities to the couriers. Why else would Willie Hebert—if that was his real name—have tried to kill them?

Despite the hot water splashing around her body, Keely shivered. Noah had been right about one thing—there was a leak in the department. Only a few people knew, or could guess, their whereabouts.

The truly horrible thought was that the informant almost certainly had to be someone she knew.

She closed her eyes and mentally ticked off anyone who knew or might have suspected that Keely and Noah were on assignment. The police chief himself, of course, although it was ludicrous to suspect Lyle Kapinski. She'd known him her entire life; he was her and Rosie's godfather.

Then there was his secretary, Erma Rodriguez. Even though she'd complained to Keely that the chief had kept mum about why Keely and Noah were in his office for so long, Keely guessed the wily woman would know all the details by now. But Erma was no international smuggler.

Still, Keely was forced to admit that Erma would have no trouble blending into the background in Mexico. Her family was from this part of Baja; she could easily obtain help if she needed it.

Besides, with those five kids to raise, Erma was always in need of money. Could her jolly demeanor be a facade?

Suddenly she heard a tap at the bathroom door. "Keely? Did you drown?"

She'd been so lost in her own thoughts she hadn't heard Noah return. Pulling the plug, she wrapped herself in a thick, thirsty towel and stepped out of the bathtub.

"Did you find some clothes?" she shouted through the bathroom door.

"Yeah, you decent?"

Once the towel was snug across her bosom, she called, "Come on in."

He walked into the steamy room and dropped a bright shopping bag on the vanity. "Lucky you look good as a Mexican peasant, since that's the only kind of clothes they sell in these hotels. Of course, you look even better in nothing." His eyebrows waggled as he stared blatantly at the shadowy V between her breasts.

"And you're a lech." With a forced smile she put her hand in the small of his back and pushed him out the door. Despite their evening of romantic ecstasy, she was feeling vulnerable and unsure. She couldn't let herself fall prey to Noah's sexy charm again; it messed up her thinking.

When she came out of the bathroom ten minutes later, dressed in another white skirt and ruffled blouse, Noah was sitting at the desk scribbling on a sheet of hotel paper.

"What are you doing?" she asked as she peeked over his shoulder.

"Still trying to figure out the most likely person to be the informant."

She laughed. "'Like minds' and all that. I was doing the same thing while I was soaking in the tub."

"Yeah? Come up with anybody interesting?"

Briefly she sketched her feelings about Chief Kapinski and Erma Rodriguez.

Noah nodded and pointed to his list. "They were numbers one and two for me, as well. I met several of your co-workers at Rosie's funeral. How about that lieutenant from vice? He was a strange bird."

She pulled up another chair. Taking his pencil, she began a mindless doodle on a hotel envelope. "Dale Cabot? He's okay, I think."

Noah shrugged. "He seemed kind of . . . intense to me."

Unsure of how much she wanted to tell him, she said simply, "We had been dating. I broke it off, he was upset. Nothing sinister."

Noah stared at her for a long time. "I'll forgo my natural male inclination to pound my chest and shout. Any particular reason you dumped him? Anything that might have bearing on this case? Other than his fancy suits, I mean."

She shook her head. "I wouldn't exactly call it 'dumping.' We weren't dating exclusively or anything. And, no, no real reason except he didn't . . ."

"Make your bells chime?"

Keely laughed wryly. "Yeah. I guess you could say that."

"Do I make your bells chime, Keely Travers?"

She wasn't about to admit that she'd never felt the rush of pure pleasure she experienced when she was with Noah.

Her mind drifted backward in time, to their younger days and the sweet sizzle of their young love.

How many times had she scrawled his name on her brown paper book covers? It was Noah who'd first taken her hand as they stood in line, waiting to go into the movies. Noah who'd given her that first tentative kiss. Noah who'd taught her to dance and to love.

It was also Noah Bannister who'd left town without a word shortly after graduation. And she couldn't allow herself to forget that hurt. Ever.

Wiping a bead of perspiration from her brow, she tried to banish the onslaught of painful recollections, but the memories had taken hold and were out of control.

She was transported back to another time, when she and Noah had been washing her father's car. He'd flicked her with a soapy sponge, and she'd retaliated by turning the hose on him, drenching him with icy water.

She could hear the echo of her teenage voice, squealing with delight as Noah had chased her around the yard. When he'd finally caught her, he'd made her do penance by kissing her until she was weak.

As a soft shudder of remembered desire overtook her, Keely blinked away the hurt. Stop it! She had to stop torturing herself.

Did he make her bells chime? Like the carillon at Westminster Cathedral. But if she kept her wits about her, he'd never know.

Chapter Fourteen

After Noah showered and changed his own clothes, they decided to have a cocktail by the pool before dinner. Noah ordered a beer for himself and a margarita for Keely.

When the drinks were served, he smeared lime over the lip of his bottle and proposed a toast. "*¡Salud!* To your health."

She clinked her glass against his and sipped the icy drink. She heard the excited squeal of some children playing in the sand. They had abandoned their sand castles and were looking out to sea. Shading her eyes with the edge of her hand, Keely followed their pointing fingers.

A school of dolphins frolicked in the surf just offshore. Framed by the pink orb of the setting sun, it was picture-postcard perfect. A paradise for lovers to laze away their evenings.

As if to remind her that they weren't lovers—at least not in the real sense—Noah said, "There was one other person I wanted to ask you about."

She damped down the disappointment that threatened to ruin her good mood. Back to business. With Noah, it seemed it was always impersonal. Had last

night only been "part of the job," as well? Had he
carried their role-playing marriage into bed?

It hurt too much to consider. Forcing herself to meet
his questioning gaze, she smiled brightly. "Who is
that?"

"That other guy I talked to at your father's. Bob
something or other."

"You can't mean Bob Craybill!"

"That's him. Why is he above suspicion?"

"He's my partner, that's why." But already doubt
had been planted in her mind. She remembered Bob's
ex-wives, his stiff spousal support payments. Suddenly he seemed all too possible.

Keely hated herself for how easily Noah lured her
into his cynical mind-set. Not everyone was guilty. Not
everyone should be suspect.

But who could they safely eliminate?

THEY DECIDED on a light supper by the pool. Afterward, a trio of street musicians wandered up and ser-
enaded them with soft Mexican love songs.

Handing the lead crooner a tip, Noah stood. "Let's
take a walk on the beach before we turn in," he suggested.

Even as he took her hand, he doubted the wisdom
of his suggestion. He'd somehow lost his perspective
on this trip. When he'd started out, he'd been certain
beyond a doubt that Rosie and Mike Travers were the
guilty parties.

Somewhere along the line, he'd kind of lost sight of
his objective. Mexico and Keely had worked their
magic on him. Charmed him into believing in goodness and integrity again. He only hoped that when this
was all over, Keely would be proven right. Suddenly he

didn't want her father or sister to be guilty of any crime.

Mostly he didn't want to be the one to break Keely's heart if his most dire suspicions came true.

Noah harbored no illusions; if he was the one who implicated either or both of her family members, Keely would never forgive him, never speak to him again.

For all he knew, their budding mutual trust could dissolve in the moonlight. But at least they still had tonight. Giving in to the need that threatened to buckle his knees, he pulled her into his arms.

Keely was startled when Noah suddenly stopped and wrapped her in his embrace. His lips on hers were warm, heavenly, and she wanted the spell he'd cast to last forever.

For despite their mutual distrust, despite their ten-year separation, despite everything, the truth was simple: she still loved Noah Bannister.

Their lips parted gently and she leaned against him, staring out into the vast emptiness of the sea. Golden moonlight dappled the softly whooshing water, creating a mood that should have been mystical. Strolling aimlessly on a deserted beach with Noah should have been enough to carry Keely away on a wave of glorious ecstasy.

But the magical evening was spoiled by the single thought that kept plaguing her. If he'd left so easily before, why should she believe that he'd stick around this time?

"Noah?"

"Hmm?"

"Can we talk?"

"I thought that's what we'd been doing."

She hesitated, afraid to spoil the gilded, fragile mood. But if they couldn't bare their innermost feelings and fears to each other, then they had nothing anyway. Taking a deep breath, she blurted out her question before she lost her nerve. "Why did you leave?"

He said nothing but released her hand and knelt in the sand, running his fingers through the satiny surf. Pointing to a cluster of rocky islets, he said, "Those must be the Coronado Islands. There used to be a lot of native goats that lived on those islands. But the military decided to use the Coronados for detonation tests and killed off all the goats."

"Why are you changing the subject?"

He stood up and handed her a smooth, shiny pebble. "I was like those goats. Living a happy, carefree existence until I was blown out of the water." He started walking back toward the jumble of rocky crags that lined the dunes.

Keely didn't follow. She stood, clutching the lacy maroon shawl around her shoulders as if it could protect her from the pain in her voice. "Noah," she called into the blustering wind. "Don't walk away. We have to talk this out."

If he heard her, he gave no notice. Finally giving up, she started walking slowly behind him. Whatever had injured him so badly ten years ago that he'd left his home and everyone he loved was still haunting him.

But it was time to stop running.

Skipping across the sand, Keely hurried toward him, determined to air out the past once and for all. She caught him just as he reached the rocky incline that led back to the hotel. "Noah, wait!"

He stopped and turned around to face her. His burnished hair, the soft, warm brown of a tattered boot, was blowing in the wind. Normally he was so perfectly groomed, so immaculate. It was as if a young, wilder Noah had stepped back into her life. She felt like crying with joy.

Running toward him, she suddenly became aware of another presence in the rocky outcropping. She stopped, static. Raising a hand, she soundlessly pointed to the obscure form.

As Noah turned to face him, the man stepped out of the shadows and pushed his hand against Noah's back. "Don't try anything funny. That's a gun in your back, Bannister."

He was dressed in dark clothing and wore a latex mask in the image of former president Reagan. Yet there was something very familiar about the way he stood, about the heft of his shoulders. And that voice, Keely thought. It sounded so familiar, and yet...it couldn't be. She didn't believe her ears. She just wouldn't accept it.

"You too, Keely. Step over where I can keep an eye on you."

Dreamlike, she stepped closer, but her trembling fingers fluttered at her mouth. There was no mistaking that voice, that bulky build. She'd known this man her entire life, and now he was threatening her. Her head swirled and she thought she would faint as her nightmare suddenly became reality.

"Chief Kapinski," she whispered. "Not you."

In response, he peeled the mask off and threw it into the rocks. "Keely, you always were too smart for your own good. Now get over here."

She moved to Noah's side. "Wh-what do you want?"

The chief laughed, a cold mirthless chuckle that chilled her to her core. "The plates, of course. Where are they?"

"In . . . in the hotel room."

"Let's go get them." He grabbed Keely's elbow and pulled her beside him, linking his arm through hers. "Feel that?"

"Yes," she whispered, too brokenhearted to say more.

"Bannister," Kapinski said, "I've got a gun on her, so don't try anything cute when we go into the hotel. I've gone too far to let anything stop me. Do we understand each other?"

Noah's voice dripped his contempt. "Yeah, Chief, I understand, all right. I have to say I never pegged you to be a slimeball who would sacrifice his own men for a little ready cash."

"No," the chief agreed. "I had you fooled, didn't I? You figured it was Mike Travers?"

Noah's silence was affirmation enough and Keely's heart ached anew.

Swallowing to dislodge the heavy lump that had settled in her throat, she said, "Let's get it over with, shall we?"

They started the slow walk back to the hotel.

Keely couldn't have been more disappointed—more heartsick—if the informant had turned out to be her own father. After all, Lyle Kapinski was her godfather and she couldn't remember when his bluff presence hadn't been a warm and loving part of her life.

Noah's arm glided around her waist and tilted her against his body as if he felt her pain and were trying to take it upon himself. But Keely couldn't gain comfort from his gesture. After all, he'd betrayed her once, as well, as deeply and as painfully as Chief Kapinski.

As their footsteps crunched on the damp sand, Keely's senses were heightened to every sound, every movement—as if she might never have the ability to feel again.

Wordlessly, they left the sand and stepped onto the flagstone pathway leading to the hotel. The sweet aroma of the night-blooming jasmine shrubs that lined the walkway added an aberrant note to the tense and frightful quiet.

"Okay, stop right here," the chief said as they came up to the door of the hotel. "Keely, come back here and stand beside me."

"Now see here, Chief—"

"Shut up, Bannister. You're as expendable as she is, so don't give me an excuse."

Keely could feel Noah tense beside her. She knew if she wasn't part of the equation, if her safety wasn't utmost in Noah's mind, he would have tackled the chief here and now. But Kapinski held all the cards and she couldn't let Noah endanger himself on her account.

She moved out of his grasp and stood next to the chief. His hand slipped behind her back and she felt a hard cylinder press against her spine. Her mind could barely process the startling realization that a man she'd known and loved all her life now held her at gunpoint.

"Okay, Bannister. Through the lobby. Nice and easy. Any sudden moves and it's Keely here who'll suffer."

"Chief," she pleaded. "You can't hope to get away with this. Once we get back to the States—"

"He doesn't plan on all of us going back," Noah interrupted. "He's planning a tragic accident in Mexico for the honeymooners, aren't you, Chief?"

"You have a big mouth, Bannister. Now open the door."

Noah swung open the heavy glass and they stepped into the hallway. They headed for the lobby, their feet melancholy echoes on the gleaming tile floor.

As they neared the lobby, the tinkle of muted voices and incongruent laughter greeted them. The chief growled out another warning as they stepped through a brightly painted archway. Other tourists milled around the grand piano in the corner, oblivious to the dreadful tableau in their midst.

The elevators were in an alcove just off the lobby. Noah pushed the button, and a moment later an elevator pinged as it approached. The door slid open and a rowdy group of college boys poured out.

"Party hearty, dude!" A large young man wearing a UC Santa Barbara T-shirt aimed a high five at Noah.

Noah pushed past him without speaking.

"Hey, whatsa matter, man? Too good to speak to a fellow countryman?"

Chief Kapinski nudged Keely into the waiting elevator. "Cool it, kid. You're drunk."

The boy slipped his foot between the doors to hold them open. Swiveling his head toward his waiting friends, he said, "Hey, guys—pops here thinks I'm drunk! What do you think?"

"I think he's right, Aaron. Come on."

The loudmouth wasn't finished. He leaned into the elevator, poked the chief in the chest and started to continue his harangue.

For the briefest of moments, Kapinski's attention was diverted. Noah seized his opportunity. With a bellow, he pushed forward, knocking the chief out of the elevator and into the startled youth weaving in the hallway.

But the mountain of a man hadn't been a police officer for thirty-odd years without honing his reaction time. In an instant he whirled around and rushed at Noah.

Thrashing like rutting bulls, the two men fell to the floor and continued pummeling each other. The youths, stunned sober, backed up and stared.

Although the chief had bulk and experience on his side, he was no match for Noah's superior strength and energy. In a short time Noah had bested the older man and turned him over onto his stomach, jerking his wrists behind his back.

"Go get the hotel security," he barked at the college boys who were still standing openmouthed. "Move it!" he shouted when they failed to respond.

Immediately the bully in the UC Santa Barbara shirt bolted for the lobby. He returned moments later, two hotel security guards in tow.

Their grasp of English was limited, but they understood enough of Noah's fractured Spanish to believe he and Keely had been assaulted by the brawny older man.

"Search him. He has a gun," Noah said.

"*¿Qué?*"

"Gun. *Pistola.*"

"Ahh." Within seconds they hauled the chief up from the floor. Although both men thoroughly searched him, no weapon was found.

Noah shook his head in bewilderment. "It has to be here. I tell you he had a gun."

The two young officers shared a disbelieving glance and ushered the entire group into the lobby.

They were met by the manager, the head of security and three members of the local police. The police officer in charge, a young man whose brass name tag identified him as Lieutenant Reseda, immediately took charge. The young officer spoke flawless English, evidence of an expensive American education.

When he heard the accusation that someone had a weapon, Reseda ordered all the men frisked. Again, no weapon was found.

After a bit of verbal wrangling, the college students were released and Noah, Keely and Kapinski were led into the security office.

The hotel security force was dismissed after turning over their facilities to Reseda. With the two other local policemen on guard outside the door, Reseda nodded toward chairs and settled himself behind the desk.

"Now, what seems to be the trouble?" he asked mildly after they were all settled in place.

Noah hooked a thumb at Kapinski. "For one thing, this guy has a gun hidden on him somewhere."

Reseda frowned. "My men already searched his body."

"Then search him again. There was no place in that elevator for him to stash a weapon. That gun didn't evaporate—he still has to be carrying."

For the first time since the altercation started, Kapinski spoke. "I don't have a gun—never did."

Keely blinked. "But you said . . . I mean, I felt it."

"May I?" Kapinski pointed to his jacket pocket and directed his question to Reseda.

"Very carefully, amigo."

Holding his sport coat open so the police officer could see what he was doing, Kapinski slowly extracted a large-diameter marking pen. Holding the implement up so that both Keely and Noah could examine it, he said, "This is what I held at your back. Keely, I'd never point a gun at you."

Reseda leaned back in the chair. "You Americans certainly keep my job from becoming too tiresome. Will someone please tell me what's going on?"

After identifying himself as a federal agent, Noah provided a rough outline of the operation in Mexico. He took care to leave out their encounter with the Ensenada police and the dead man in their hotel room.

When Noah had finished, Reseda said, "Exactly where are these alleged counterfeiting plates?"

Noah hooked a thumb in the direction of the lobby. "Locked in the hotel safe."

Reseda nodded. "I'll want to look at them later. But right now let's clear up the matter at hand. You say you have no identification to support your claim?"

"No," Noah admitted. "Because we were on a covert operation, I didn't think it would be wise to carry anything that might blow our cover."

"I see." Reseda turned to the chief. "And you are a police official with the San Diego Police Department?"

"That's right." Kapinski flipped a leather wallet holding his badge and identification card onto the desk.

Reseda examined it carefully and handed the wallet back. He turned to face Keely for the first time. "Miss Travers, is it? You say you are also a member of the San Diego Police Department?"

"That's right."

"May I see your identification, please?"

She forced a disarming smile. "I'm afraid I don't have any with me. Only credit cards."

"Oh, yes, the covert operation with Mr. Bannister."

"That's right."

Reseda leaned back in his chair and stared at the ceiling. After a moment he spun around and addressed Kapinski. "So, Chief Kapinski, for the moment we'll leave aside the matter of your not having any jurisdiction in my country and discuss your role in tonight's events. Is it true that you attempted to steal illegal counterfeiting equipment from Agent Bannister?"

"Sort of." He shrugged.

"Sort of? Could you perhaps explain?"

Kapinski, who suddenly looked twenty years older, leaned forward and peered around Noah, fastening his gaze on Keely. "Honey, you have to believe I never would have hurt you."

"What about Willie Hebert?" Noah demanded. "I don't suppose you hurt him, either?"

"Who's Willie Hebert?" The chief looked confused, as if he truly didn't know what Noah was talking about.

"It doesn't matter," Keely said quickly. Noah hadn't mentioned the dead man in his recitation to Reseda. She knew that only his anger at Kapinski for putting her into jeopardy had caused him to blurt out the man's name just now.

Reseda tapped the desktop with a pencil. "Ms. Travers, if you are attempting to conceal the murder of an American tourist at the La Posada del Sol, don't bother. I know all about Mr. Hebert."

She blushed. "I'm sorry, Lieutenant."

His pencil tapped faster. "And, of course, you and Mr. Bannister were in no way responsible for Mr. Hebert's death?"

"Certainly not! We should have told you. He broke into our room with a gun, but we got away. We think he was looking for the plates." She paused for breath. "Anyway, the next morning when we returned, he was dead. We had nothing to do with it."

Reseda chewed on his upper lip for a while, then said, "I may be a fool, but I'm inclined to believe you. In fact, Captain Suarez of the Ensenada police has a woman, purportedly Mr. Hebert's wife, in custody. She, of course, also denies any involvement in his death. But Captain Suarez finds it interesting that she didn't report him missing. So, for the moment, I'll accept your story. Go on, please."

To give herself time to absorb Reseda's startling news, she continued questioning Kapinski. "You said you wouldn't hurt me, but you wanted those plates. Are you telling me that you aren't involved with that counterfeiting syndicate?"

"Oh, Keely, I'm so embarrassed. Of course I'm not a counterfeiter." Tears in his eyes, the older man explained in a broken voice that he'd received a report of their troubles in Ensenada through official channels. Fearful they might be inmates in a Mexican jail, he'd touched bases with Noah's partner in Washington.

Not knowing Kapinski's relationship with the Travers family, Noah's partner had let it slip that Noah's prime suspect was Mike Travers. The man said that Noah was convinced Travers was the informant and was using either one or both of his daughters to cover his own reprehensible tracks.

"That's ridiculous! My father is an honest man."

Kapinski nodded sadly. "I know that, but after Bannister's partner got through listing all the circumstantial evidence they've piled up, I knew we'd never be able to prove his innocence." He stopped as his eyes filled and his voice grew husky with unshed tears. "Your father is like a brother to me and I'd do anything to keep him from suffering anymore."

Noah said slowly, "Including setting yourself up as the culprit to deflect suspicion from Mike."

"Anything," Kapinski said forcefully.

Suddenly Keely understood that the police captain had offered himself as a sacrifice to save her father. Her own eyes damp with tears of overwhelming gratitude, she jumped out of her chair and threw her arms around Kapinski's bulky frame. "Oh, Chief! How could I ever have doubted you? I'm so sorry. But... but my dad is innocent. I'd bet my life on it."

Kapinski dabbed at his eyes and patted her shoulder. "Me too, honey, me too."

Keely straightened up and turned to Noah, her hands on her hips in an unconscious show of her determination. "You say my father's guilty, and we know he isn't. Seems to me that we're at an impasse, Bannister."

"Seems like."

"Then let's settle this once and for all."

Noah rubbed at the dark blush of whiskers along his jawline. "And I suppose you've come up with a plan?"

"Yes. Sort of."

She hesitated, staring at the three men. Would they go along with her scheme? Everything she held dear depended on her ability to convince these men to help her. But if her plan failed, all would be lost.

Taking a deep breath, Keely laid out her plan.

They would leave the package containing the real engraving plates in Lieutenant Reseda's custody. Chief Kapinski would return to San Diego and leak word of their whereabouts to several people in the department.

"Maybe he could even say that Noah was arrested in Ensenada. That way the informant would think I was alone. Easier prey."

"You mean set yourself up as bait, don't you?" Noah asked in an incredulous voice.

"Do you have a better plan?" she countered. "Hear me out." She continued with her rough outline.

Using the fake package as bait, Noah and Keely would wait in Rosarito and see who came after them.

"Absolutely not," Noah said, tossing his head. "It's too dangerous. You're proposing to be a sitting duck for a murderer. I can't allow it."

"It's not your decision to make," she stated calmly.

He continued to shake his head. "There are too many holes, too many things that can go wrong."

Keely refused to relent. It wasn't foolproof, she admitted, but it was the best they had.

"At least this will prove once and for all that my father is innocent. And we stand a pretty good chance of finding the murderer."

Noah's gaze bored into her for an endless moment, until at last he stood up. "Well, Chief. While you and I have been operating on testosterone, Keely's used her brain. I don't know about you, but I'm willing to give her plan a try."

She smiled up at him gratefully. Knowing that he still believed in her father's guilt, she was even more touched that he was trying to keep an open mind—willing to be convinced.

Perhaps even more poignant was his faith in her professional ability. By agreeing to her plan, he was placing the success of this entire operation squarely on her shoulders. If she goofed, all his work for the past two years would disappear down the proverbial porcelain bowl.

She vowed not to let him down. Both of their futures depended on her identifying and apprehending the real informant.

The chief rose to his feet. "Okay, I'm game."

The three of them turned and faced Lieutenant Reseda. They were in his country, under his jurisdiction. If he decided to hold them or press charges, it was all over.

He returned their stares for a protracted moment, then nodded slowly. "All right, Ms. Travers. Let's try your plan."

As the three men huddled over the desk ironing out the details, she suddenly felt weak and frightened inside.

She was betting everything on her father's innocence. Keely knew her plan was a gamble—a desperate gamble.

She only prayed it would work.

Chapter Fifteen

Keely and Noah headed up to their room shortly after Lyle Kapinski left.

Both of them were quiet, pensive, as if neither wanted to broach the subject of what would happen tomorrow. Because, Keely thought, tomorrow it would be all over. One way or another, they'd know the truth.

Once the chief leaked word of her "dilemma" in Mexico, the real criminal in the department would surely make his or her appearance. As her father always said, turn on the lights and watch the cockroaches scuttle.

If all went well, the new day would bring an end to the speculation about her family's involvement. Would the real killer prove Rosie's innocence, or add weight to the evidence of her guilt?

But tomorrow held another bittersweet promise. This was the last night of her assignment with Noah. Would he give her a polite kiss goodbye in the morning and head back to D.C., or would he want to continue the fragile relationship they'd started this week?

Tomorrow would tell its own story. Tonight, all they could do was wait.

When they reached their hotel room, Noah pulled off his shoes and flopped onto the bed. He lay with his arm over his eyes, shielding her from whatever he was feeling.

Keely kicked off her sandals and curled up in the armchair, watching him. Whatever he was thinking about must have been taking considerable concentration, she thought, watching his jaw muscles work as if he were chewing on a buffalo hide.

She got up and walked over to the window. It was hot, terribly still. As if the night, too, were waiting for something to happen. She stood looking out at the moonlight dancing on the ocean, and suddenly felt as alone as a single fish in that great stretch of endless sea.

So lost in her own thoughts that she didn't hear him get out of bed, Keely was nevertheless not surprised when she felt his presence directly behind her.

"Come here," he whispered against the back of her head, and slipped his arms around her waist, pulling her against him. They stood joined for a long while, until slowly he turned her around to face him.

He took her against him and hungrily kissed her.

Her hands skimmed over the broad plane of his back as she clung to him, desperate to somehow make him hers—if only for the night. She pressed against him and felt the hard strength of his excitement.

Her knees wobbled and she began to tremble as his mouth continued to claim hers. He whirled her in a circle and walked her backward to the bed.

He smiled slowly and lifted his eyebrows. "Do you know what I'm thinking right now? What I want more than anything in the world?"

She had a pretty good idea what he was leading up to, but feeling suddenly giddy and girlish, she tossed her head, needing to hear him say the words. "No, what?" she breathed.

His lips tipped again, in the sexiest, most enticing grin she had ever seen. "I want to make love to you. Slowly, deliberately and with complete attention to... *all* the details." His fingertips flicked down her arms and tiny bumps of gooseflesh quivered in the wake of his touch.

With a tortured groan, he dropped his hand to the scoop of her blouse. He untied the small white cord that held the peasant blouse on her shoulders. As the fabric loosened its hold, he used his fingers to trail along the edge of the cotton, teasing her tender flesh and sending hot rushes of desire racing through her body.

Lowering his head, he kissed her deeply while his hand slipped beneath the fabric. He gently caressed her breast, his fingertip finding and teasing her sensitive peak.

Keely knew that she was taking a great risk. When they'd made love before, it had been a spontaneous joining, a curiosity even, to rediscover a past that had eluded them. This was different. This was deliberate. A conscious decision on her part. And it could break her heart.

But her traitorous body was past caring. In a desperate sudden need to feel his naked skin against her own, she smoothed her hands up the broad expanse of his chest and prized open his shirt. Her searching hands glided along the firm planes of his heaving chest, down to the taut muscles of his stomach.

At her touch, Noah's kisses grew hungrier, so hungry that she shuddered in luxurious anticipation. Her entire being existed only for his touch. "You are the most beautiful, most desirable woman I've ever known," he whispered against her neck. "God, I could never get you out of my system. Never."

Her last doubt deserted her as his words touched and thrilled her. She wanted to melt into him, to allow the liquid center of her femininity to meld around his hardness. Her need suddenly a living, gripping entity that threatened to take over her soul, Keely pressed against him.

Noah pulled back then and stared at her in the moonlight, his expression at once demanding and unfathomable. Then, wordlessly, he reached down and knuckled the tender flesh of her lower lip and Keely felt the delicious beginnings of a dull throbbing that wanted, no, demanded, him.

With a few deft movements, he had skimmed her blouse and skirt aside.

With an enticing slowness, his fingers slipped beneath the silky wisp of her bra, sliding the strap down her shoulder.

Cupping her face in his hands, he lowered his lips to hers in a kiss of incredible sweetness, as he gently lowered her onto the bed.

Her senses were aflame as his fingertips gently grazed the soft flesh of her thighs. She quivered and squirmed on the bed, until at last he raised up to meet her lips with his. Her need threatened to overwhelm her and, with trembling fingers, she reached for him, but he grabbed her wrists and held her arms above her head while his lips continued their exquisite torture.

In that moment Keely understood that no matter what divergent paths their tomorrows might take, she would always have this night. But if she lived a million years, no other man would ever make her body sing with such glorious abandon. She felt a moment's loss for the empty nights of her future, but she would always have this moment to remember, to cling to.

He was gentle, yet thorough, and she thought she might scream with her need. If they only had this one night left to them, he seemed determined to give her a night she'd never forget. When at last he took her, she felt an explosion from the very depths of her soul.

In that moment Keely knew with a sorrowful certainty that no other man would ever thrill her as Noah did. She wept softly for all the years they'd lost. Both in the past and possibly in the future.

THE NEXT MORNING Keely went downstairs to breakfast alone. Nodding pleasantly to the headwaiter, she chose a patio table overlooking the ocean.

She sipped the strong Mexican coffee and nibbled at a local specialty, lobster machaca, a delicious blend of scrambled eggs, vegetables and chunks of succulent lobster.

She broke off a piece of tortilla and was scooping a spoonful of the egg mixture onto the flat bread when a shadow fell across the table. She looked up.

Lieutenant Dale Cabot, her former boyfriend and superior in Vice, was standing beside her. "Hi, Keely. Mind if I sit down?"

Without waiting for an answer, he pulled out a chair and called to the waiter. "Can I have a cup of coffee over here, pardner?"

Acting as nonchalant as if they had planned the meeting, he reached into the bread basket and pulled out a roll. He smeared butter onto the sweet Mexican bread and accepted a mug of coffee from the waiter. "So, Keely, where's the boyfriend?"

Having suddenly lost her appetite, she pushed her machaca aside and leaned back in her chair. "He's, uh, tied up right now, Dale. What are you doing here?"

He munched on the roll and wiped a smear of buttery crumbs from his lips with the back of his hand. "I'm here on a mercy mission. Chief sent me to bring you home."

She ran a fingertip around the edge of her cup and eyed him thoughtfully. Her mind wouldn't accept the reality that Dale Cabot, the man who'd pledged his love for her, was a murderer. Perhaps the chief really had changed his mind and sent Dale to retrieve them. She had to know for certain. "I don't understand. How did you know where to find me?"

He swallowed the rest of his roll. "I told you—the chief sent me to escort you, and the package, back across the border."

"I see. I'm on vacation, Dale. I don't really need an escort."

"Sure you are," he grunted. "And I'm sure Bannister's having a real good time in the Ensenada jail."

There it was—the confirmation she'd needed. If the chief had changed his mind, he would never have told Dale that Noah was in jail. There would have been no reason to. The only reason they'd started that rumor was so that the informant would think Keely was alone and vulnerable.

And Dale Cabot had taken the bait.

She started to push her chair back, but he reached out and clasped his hand over hers. "What's your hurry? Finish your breakfast."

"I—I'm not very hungry." Her skin crawled beneath his palm, as if a snake had suddenly slithered over her flesh.

"Sit down, finish your coffee. Traffic's a bitch at the border right now. We've got lots of time."

Although Keely's every instinct urged her to flee, she slowly sank back down.

Dale drained his mug and waved it high in the air, signaling to the waiter for more coffee. "How about you, want some more?"

"No. Thanks." To keep her voice civil required monumental effort. This was the man who'd brought so much pain and grief to her family. He'd known all about Rosie's gambling—thanks to Keely's shared confidence—and had used the information to snare Rosie into helping transport illegal goods. Then he'd planted false rumors about her father. Maybe he'd even had a hand in Rosie's death.

The thought that she'd danced with him, even allowed him to kiss her, caused Keely to shudder in repugnance.

"What's the matter? You cold? We could go up to your room for a while."

"No!" she answered quickly. Just the mental image of being alone in a room with Dale Cabot made her feel claustrophobic. "I mean, I'm fine."

He leaned forward and plucked a daisy out of the small bud vase in the center of the table. He pulled off a petal. Then another. "She loves me. She loves me not. Why don't you love me, Keely?"

"I, uh, I really don't think this is the appropriate time or place to discuss—"

"I always loved you," he interrupted. He picked off another petal. Then two. "She loves me. She loves me not. I always treated you well, Keely. Not like Bannister. Yet you always wanted him. Why is that? You know, I don't understand you sometimes, Keely."

Dale didn't understand her! Sometimes she didn't understand herself. The unvarnished truth was that she was holding out for bells and whistles, a man who made her toes curl when he kissed her.

Noah Bannister curled her toes.

But she couldn't say that to Dale Cabot. He was nervous, tapping the tabletop and plucking at the flower. She saw him suddenly in a new and frightening light. He was a man on the edge, one who might explode with very little provocation.

Rather than push him further, she changed the subject. "You never told me why the chief sent you. My vacation isn't over yet. I was going to stay on for a few more days."

"Sure," he snorted, squashing the daisy in his large hand. "Sure you were. You were gonna stay until you could bail Bannister out of jail."

"Dale, my relationship with Noah has nothing to do with you. So why should I cut my vacation short?"

He stood up and threw a wad of crumpled bills onto the table. "I wasn't going to tell you until we were across the border, but your father's been taken ill. Chief says you should come right away, and bring the package."

"Oh my god—not Dad!" She jumped to her feet and picked up her purse. "We'd better hurry."

She had wondered what ruse Dale would come up with if she faltered, and like a trained assassin, he'd aimed directly for her most vulnerable spot. Even knowing it was a lie, her heart still pounded with anxiety. Dale Cabot was a desperate man. There didn't seem to be any depth to which he wouldn't sink to achieve his end.

Leading the way into the lobby, she said, "The package is in the hotel safe."

He followed close on her heels as she walked toward the registration desk. The "clerk" on duty was Lieutenant Reseda. But he scarcely made eye contact when Keely handed him her claim check. A moment later he returned with the package. "Will there be anything else, Ms. Travers?"

"No, that's all. Thank you."

"Don't you have to check out, pay your bill?" Dale asked, taking the parcel from her hands.

"No. I paid when I checked in. I'm ready to go."

"What about your luggage?"

She shrugged. "Everything got left on the ship. This is it."

"Good. My car's in the parking lot. Let's go."

Out of the corner of her eye, she saw Reseda pick up the in-house telephone. As per their arrangement, he was calling Noah in the bar to let him know it was going down.

Stalling in order to give Noah time to follow them, she said, "You brought your car down here? Your prized Mustang?"

"Nah. I rented a car."

"What kind?"

He stopped cold and stared at her. "What does it matter? What's going on, Keely—is this a setup?"

"I don't know what you're talking about."

Grasping her roughly by the elbow, he hurried her toward the door. "Let's get the hell out of here."

Outside, he took a quick look around and hustled her to the parking lot. Stopping at a blue sedan, he opened the door and pushed her into the passenger seat. He rushed around to the driver's side and slipped behind the wheel. He started the engine, and with an ear-splitting scream of tires spinning on gravel, sped out of the parking lot.

A moment later they were in heavy traffic heading for the border crossing at San Ysidro.

While they plodded along the rutted side streets of Tijuana, Keely tried several times to glance in the rearview mirror to see if Lieutenant Reseda and Noah were behind them. With the hundreds of cars clotting the narrow thoroughfares, it was impossible to tell.

She might very well be on her own with a killer.

At last they reached the border. She glanced at Dale. Even though it was a mild morning, a bright sheen of perspiration shone on his face and his breathing was hard and jagged. During the ride he'd been almost silent, only speaking occasionally to mutter imprecations to other drivers. He hadn't uttered a single word to Keely since they'd left Rosarito.

The strain between them was a throbbing, palpable entity, a third being in the car.

As the other vehicles in front of them inched toward the Border Patrol officers at the checkpoint, she tried again to peek into the rearview mirror.

"Who are you looking for—your boyfriend, Bannister?" His voice was as loud and disconcerting as a shotgun blast.

"I was just looking to see how much traffic is behind us."

He grunted noncommittally and inched forward. There was only one car remaining in line ahead of the them. Soon they would be back in the States. Whatever move he had in mind would be coming soon.

A shiver of apprehension raced down her backbone. She closed her eyes in a silent prayer that the border guards wouldn't stop Noah and Lieutenant Reseda.

The car ahead of them pulled out and the guard waved them forward. Dale eased forward a few feet and rolled down his window. "Morning, officer."

The Border Patrol agent was a woman, sturdy and competent looking in her olive green uniform. "Hi, folks. What's your citizenship?"

"U.S.," they answered in unison.

The guard's eyes scanned the interior of the car with a practiced motion. "What are you bringing back today? Any alcohol?"

"Not a thing," Dale said with an affable smile. "We just went over for a breakfast on the ocean."

The guard smiled back and waved them through. Keely had forgotten what a devastating effect he often had on women.

A moment later they were back in the U.S.

"CAN'T YOU GO any faster?" Noah demanded as the blue sedan disappeared from sight.

"Would you like me to go over or through these other cars?" Reseda countered as he calmly maneuvered through the heavy traffic. "We'll catch them at the border. Everyone's been alerted."

Noah leaned back in the car seat and tried to force himself to relax. But Keely was alone with a murderer and he was stalled in traffic. He'd been a fool to let her talk him into this crazy scheme in the first place. Sure, she was a trained police officer and, under most circumstances, more than able to fend off a physical attack.

Unfortunately, this time her opponent was also an expert in martial arts. And Noah had no doubt he was armed and extremely dangerous. If Cabot thought he was being double-crossed, Keely's life wouldn't be worth a peso on the open market.

The light changed and Reseda surged ahead of the rumbling truck that had been keeping them back. Turning down a side street, he drove like a demon along the cobbled road, then turned again, and again, until Noah was completely disoriented. "Where are you going?"

Reseda grinned and winked. "Shortcut." He angled down an alley that was so narrow that Noah knew a skateboard wouldn't fit through. Reseda wasn't daunted by the lack of space. Easing the left tires up onto the sidewalk, he bypassed a car parked in the alley and swerved around a corner.

When Noah opened his eyes again, they were at the border.

He leaned his head out the window and stared at the slow, congested lines of traffic waiting their turn to cross. Finally he spotted the blue sedan. "Lane six!" he shouted, and pulled his head back inside just as Reseda cut into the lane beside them.

There were still at least a half-dozen cars between them and Keely.

Noah knew that as soon as Cabot crossed through to the other side, he'd have a six-lane freeway at his disposal. He could disappear with Keely and they'd never find him. "Come on, come on," Noah muttered to the slow-moving traffic.

Then he saw Cabot's car pull between the guard's stanchions. In an instant he was out of sight.

There was nothing they could do except wait their turn and inch forward, one excruciating car length at a time. Suddenly Reseda shouted, "Hang on, gringo!" and jerked out of line.

His experienced eye had noted a new lane opening up and he expertly guided his cruiser to the gate. As they pulled up beside the bewildered Border Patrol agent, Noah glimpsed Chief Kapinski standing in the shade a few feet away.

"Looks like the cavalry has arrived," Reseda said, nodding toward Kapinski.

Noah opened the car door and slid out. "Hey, Reseda, I, uh, I really want to thank you for all your help. I don't know—"

"Well, what're you waiting for? Go save that gorgeous woman. And name your first kid after me."

"You got it, amigo." Noah darted toward Chief Kapinski.

"Sir! This isn't a pedestrian exit," the guard protested as he trotted past.

Kapinski stepped forward and flashed his badge. "Police business, officer. This man's with me."

"If you say so, sir."

"I do say so." Turning to Noah, he flipped the younger man a set of car keys. "You drive and I'll navigate. They were just spotted driving down Dairy Mart Road. Know where that is?''

''Sure do. We used to drag race out there when I was in high school.''

''Now why doesn't that surprise me?'' the chief muttered as Noah slid behind the wheel. Within seconds they pulled into the flow of traffic heading north toward San Diego.

THEY'D ONLY DRIVEN a short distance when Dale took an exit ramp off the freeway. Still playing her part as the distraught daughter, Keely asked, ''Where are we going? There's no hospital out here.''

In fact, there was nothing out here, if her memory was correct. This area was so deserted it was a prime thruway for the transportation of illegal aliens into the United States. Every night, the ''coyotes''—smugglers of human flesh—delivered their hapless victims to this empty stretch of wilderness and left them on their own to make their way north.

As a police officer, Keely knew that these poor, uneducated farmers from the interior were often robbed and even killed by the same men they'd paid exorbitant sums to help them. Sometimes their bodies lay undiscovered for days, even weeks in these desolate fields.

Suddenly her apprehension escalated into pure horror. Dale Cabot meant to kill her and dump her body in the brush that grew waist high in these parts.

The realization was paralyzing. But Keely refused to admit defeat. She wouldn't make it easy for him. She also knew that Noah, and any help he might bring, might as well be light-years away. If she was going to live long enough to see another sunset, she would have to save herself.

As if sensing her sudden awareness, Dale pulled the car over to the side of the road and stopped. Drawing his police revolver from beneath his jacket, he said coldly, "Well, looks like the end of the line, Keely. Let's go for a little walk."

Stalling, she shook her head as if she didn't understand what was happening. "What are you doing, Dale?"

He laughed mirthlessly. "You know, you're not a bad actor, Keely. In fact, if you'd chosen the stage instead of police work, you might have had a long, happy little life."

She didn't have to fake the terror that was stalking her heart, turning her insides to quivering jelly. "But why, Dale?"

"Why? Don't be such a fool! Now get out of the car."

Ignoring his order, she said, "What would make an honest cop turn, Dale? Tell me."

"The money, of course. I've always needed a lot of money to live the life I wanted. You know that."

And so she did. She thought back to all the signs— the expensive clothing, the fancy apartment she knew he could ill afford. Even his treasured Mustang was an expensive collector's model. Everything about Dale Cabot shrieked of his love of money. Why, oh why, hadn't she seen it earlier?

He nudged her with the gun barrel and she opened the car door and slid out. His own door slammed loudly. Then he was walking toward her.

Behind him, in the distance, she saw a tiny speck on the road, a speck that grew slightly larger as she watched. Could that be a car approaching? Noah? *Oh, God, please let it be Noah,* she prayed silently.

She kept her eyes on the dark flash on the horizon. Yes! It *was* a car, and it was moving fast.

To distract Dale, and keep herself alive a few moments longer, she waited until he was beside her and said, "At least tell me why. I think you owe me that much."

"I don't owe you a damn thing, but I told you—the money they offered beat the hell out of my salary."

"No. I mean why me, why my sister—my father?"

He laughed again. A callous, ugly chortle that made her flesh creep. "Because you were so easy, Keely. You told me all your family secrets. You were a chicken just waiting to be plucked."

"But why involve Rosie?"

"I needed her. She was so easy to blackmail. I stole one of your deposit slips from your purse, then all I had to do was deposit a little money into your account and show your sister. I told her your reputation and your career as a cop would be ruined if she didn't go along with me. I even convinced her it was all her fault." He paused, his expression stormy. "You should have loved me back, Keely. I told you that you'd be sorry."

No, for once she was anything but sorry. In her lifetime, Keely had loved and been hurt by those she cared about the most. She'd been wrong, as well. She should have trusted her sister, and the chief. And all those years ago, she should have trusted Noah.

Her instincts had been right on target when it came to the devastatingly handsome Dale Cabot, however. And if dying was the price she paid for not falling for his practiced line, then so be it. Her only regret was that she might not live long enough to tell Noah how wrong she'd been, and that she still loved him.

She raised her chin and stared into his cold, spiritless eyes. "You're a snake, Dale Cabot, and a disgrace to your badge. I couldn't love you if we were the only survivors of a nuclear holocaust."

His face reddened with rage and hate filled his eyes.

She felt polluted by his venom and allowed her gaze to flicker over his shoulder.

The blur on the road behind him had taken on a shape now, and she could make out the distinct features of a car. Two shadowy figures were visible behind the windshield. Fearful of attracting Dale's attention to the speeding auto, she looked away from the mesmerizing image and focused again on her captor. "One thing I don't understand."

"Keep walking." They crunched along the sandy soil, between patches of chaparral and around spiny cactus. When they'd gone a dozen yards from the road, he said, "There's lots you don't understand, babe. What in particular?"

"Why did you kill Willie Hebert? Wasn't he working with you?"

"That fool, Hebert!" Dale spit out the name as if he'd tasted something vile. "He was supposed to stick to you and Bannister until the plates were safely back across the border and in my hands. The idiot lost track of you for a full day. He was, shall we say, eliminated, because he failed in his simple job. These plates are worth millions. My employers don't tolerate incompetence. Or witnesses.''

The car was coming up close now. So near she could make out the faint whir of its tires on the pavement.

"This is far enough, I think." He turned around to gauge the distance between them and the road and spied the car speeding in their direction. "You bitch! You set me up."

He lunged for her but Keely sidestepped and pretended to fall. Scooping up a double handful of the gritty dirt, she leapt up and pitched both handfuls into Cabot's eyes, momentarily blinding him.

"I'll kill you," he screamed, swiping his hands across his face.

In the distance, Keely heard the car screech to a halt, but all she could see was the barrel of Dale Cabot's revolver, aimed directly at her heart.

NOAH PULLED UP to the curb in a squeal of brakes and threw open the door. Cabot and Keely were out in the brush, facing each other. He didn't need the eyesight of an eagle to see the gun pointing at her.

Fueled by fear and adrenaline, Noah bolted across the empty field. His mind screamed with the vision of a thousand horrors, all of them involving losing Keely. God, he had to reach her in time, he just had to.

As he drew closer, he saw Cabot glance his way. As if in slow motion, Noah saw the ragged fury on the man's face, saw him swing back around and point the weapon at Keely.

With the mindless ferocity of a submachine gun, Noah flew across the desert, his feet raising tiny dust devils as he lightly touched ground.

He could see Cabot's jaw clench, his knuckles whiten as he lifted his gun higher. He was going to shoot her!

With a last flying leap, Noah covered the remaining few feet and barreled into him just as the weapon discharged. The roar was deafening, its impact immediate. Like a beautiful doe, brought down by a high-powered rifle, Keely slumped to the ground.

Chapter Sixteen

Cabot was writhing on the ground. Consumed by rage, Noah pounced, subduing the man in scant seconds. He wanted to beat Cabot until his fists were raw and bloody, but he couldn't allow himself the luxury. Keely needed his help.

Chief Kapinski puffed up and knelt at her side. "She's still alive," he shouted, "But I don't know for how long."

Noah rolled the unconscious villain over until he was facedown in the sand. He waited until Kapinski pulled out his handcuffs before he stood up and let the older man subdue their prisoner.

Quickly closing the gap between them, Noah dropped to his knees beside Keely. Her pretty white blouse was stained a bright crimson. There was so much blood, it didn't seem possible that she could survive. Ripping off his own shirt, Noah rolled it into a ball and pressed it against her chest to stanch the flow of blood.

At that moment several police cars, sirens blaring, pulled up.

As Mike Travers and his retinue of fellow officers raced across the sand, Noah screamed, "Get an ambulance! No, call for a helicopter! Keely's been shot!"

Mike Travers's steps faltered, but he turned to bark an order to a uniformed policeman before he loped toward his daughter.

He knelt in the sand beside Noah, who was cradling the injured woman in his arms. Damp tracks glimmered down Noah's face as he whispered, "Hang on, Keely. Don't leave me now, hang on. I couldn't stand to lose you again. Please don't leave me."

But she was so pale. So frightfully pale.

SHE WAS IN SURGERY for nearly four hours. Tense, endless hours in which Noah did nothing but reflect on the emptiness of his life. And pray for Keely.

What a damned fool he'd been all these years. Blaming her for not taking his side, for not standing up for him. But he'd never taken her into his confidence. Never trusted her enough to tell her what was really going on.

He'd been too young, too full of the importance of the role that had been thrust upon him. When everything had fallen apart, he'd taken all of his anger, his disappointment, out on Keely.

Like a callous fool, he'd left town without saying a word.

She'll be sorry when I'm gone. He could almost hear the younger Noah's self-pitying thoughts.

Now, though, he understood the selfish motivations of his youth. What he'd wanted, of course, was for her to somehow follow him. Maybe she was supposed to have begged his mother or Todd for information. He had expected her to demonstrate her love by finding him.

He'd demonstrated his love by abandoning her.

What a jerk he'd been.

But if he was given a second chance, Noah swore he'd somehow make it all up to her. He'd screwed up their past, but maybe, just maybe, they could have a future.

He looked up as Mike Travers trudged in carrying two cups of coffee. "Any word yet?"

Noah shook his head as he gratefully accepted a cup and swallowed the hot, fragrant brew. "No. No one's been in. How long has it been, Mike?"

The old man didn't even glance at his watch. "Only a little while, son."

"I couldn't bear to lose her, Mike." His voice broke and he took refuge in the bitter coffee. He should be the one offering support to the older man, but Noah felt helpless against the impotent fear that shuddered through his body when he remembered the dreadful blast of that gun.

If only he'd driven a little faster. If only he'd run harder when he got out of the car. If only...

"Son?" Mike's withered hand clamped around his forearm.

Noah looked up. A doctor, still wearing his sweat-stained scrub uniform, stood in the doorway.

"You folks Ms. Travers's family?"

"Yes," they answered together.

The surgeon stepped into the room and nodded. "She lost a lot of blood, but she sure has a strong will to live. Go home and get some rest, fellas. Your lady's going to be just fine."

With a whoop of joy, Noah leapt to his feet and threw his arms around Mike. "When can we see her?"

"She's in recovery now. She won't know a thing until sometime tomorrow. Go home and sleep. She'll be wanting some company in the morning."

After they both offered their heartfelt thanks, Noah draped an arm around Mike's thin shoulders and walked him to the car. They, too, had some past to clear up, but everything could wait until morning.

Keely was going to be fine.

"WHATEVER YOU DO, don't make me laugh," Keely muttered the next morning when the two men ambled into her room, arms laden with stuffed toys and about a thousand balloons.

Moving to either side of her hospital bed, each man staked his claim. While Mike held the hand that didn't have the IV hookup, Noah smoothed her soft dark hair from her forehead.

"You really had us worried, sweetheart."

"You saved my life again, Noah. I—I can never repay you."

"No." He shook his head for emphasis. "I never should have let you leave the hotel with him. You were the one that took all the chances. I saw you arguing with that bastard, distracting him. You're the hero, Keely."

Mike swiped at a damp spot under his eyes. "Stop it, both of you. Can't abide all this sentimental pap."

"Sure, Pop." She curled her fingertips in his. But her gaze was fastened to blue-gray eyes. She could drown in the softness she saw in their depths. "Anyway, how did everything end up? Did we make a righteous arrest?"

Noah nodded. "Sure did. According to your buddy Bob Craybill, a search of Marty Sargent's office turned up all the evidence we need to put Cabot behind bars for a very long time—although he's already singing to the D.A. He wants to barter for a lighter sentence in exchange for testifying against the syndicate."

"That's wonderful." She motioned for another drink of water. When she'd finished, she asked, "What about Florence Hebert?"

Noah brushed his fingertips across the soft plane of Keely's cheek. He couldn't seem to touch her enough. In fact, when she got out of the hospital he intended to touch every square inch of her—very carefully. If she ever forgave him.

"Noah?" Her warm brown eyes were searching. "Have you checked out into never-never land?"

"Sorry. What did you ask?"

"About Florence Hebert?"

"Oh, that's right. We already said she was in custody. She dropped out of sight since her release from the Ensenada police. I don't think she'll get far though. Since Cabot's singing like a songbird, it's only a matter of time until they catch up with her. I think she was a little out of her element in Mexico, anyway."

Keely chuckled. "I know what you mean. Her polyester pantsuits kind of stood out in the crowd."

"Well, I'll tell you one thing, little lady," her father chimed in. "I don't want you going on anymore undercover work. My old ticker can't take the strain."

She suddenly sobered. "You know what scares me the most? The fact that we all worked with Dale Cabot for years and didn't have an inkling he was involved with an illegal gambling syndicate. Gives me the shivers just thinking about how many times I was alone with him."

Noah leaned over and kissed a strand of black hair that tickled her forehead. "Don't worry, Keely, you'll never have to be alone with that creep again."

She smiled up at him and signaled for another sip of water. "You know, he told me he blackmailed Rosie into helping him. She only agreed because of me and that money in my account." She stared beseechingly at Noah, begging him to believe her.

"Neither one of my daughters would willingly break the law," Mike said staunchly.

"You're right," Noah agreed. "According to Cabot's confession, Rosie changed her mind. She threatened to go to the police with everything she knew about Sargent and the entire operation. Cabot told his boss, who instructed him to cause the accident."

"That bastard!" Mike indulged in a rare profanity. "If I ever see him again outside a courtroom, I'll..." His voice drifted off as he was overcome with emotion.

It was obvious that knowing a fellow policeman had been responsible for the murder of his youngest child was almost more than the older man could absorb.

Keely gestured for the glass of water on the bedside stand. With Noah's help, she sipped through the glass straw. She dropped her head back onto the pillow. "But why did Sargent involve Rosie in the first place?"

Her father picked up the narrative. "Like we suspected earlier, honey. Rosie had been gambling again and had a pretty steep debt. Realizing she'd be a risk-free courier, Sargent coerced her into agreeing to smuggle the plates into the country. Apparently he had no idea that she had any connection to the police department. And when she told him...well, I guess that ultimately led to her death."

"But she wasn't going to go through with it, Pop. We have to hold on to that."

"You're right," he said, nodding. "At least that's something. Listen, I've got an appointment with that witch doctor in oncology. Can I trust you young folks by yourselves for a while?"

Noah laughed and pointed to all the medical hookups attached to her body. "I'd say she's going to be tied up right here, Mike."

After Keely's father made his exit, Noah closed the door behind him. Pulling a metal chair to her bedside, he said, "Feel up to a serious talk?"

"About what?" she murmured. "I thought we had the case all settled."

"Not about the case, about us."

"Us?" There was that squeak again.

"Yeah. I think it's time we hashed out the past. See where the future's going to take us."

She drew a deep breath. "Okay, I'll go first. I have to admit, when you started having problems, you know, fighting in school, scuffles with the law, I didn't know what to think."

He started to interrupt, but she held up her hand. "Let me finish. Although my dad kept making excuses for you, I was frightened by your rebellious spirit. Knowing how your father got into trouble with his drinking, I was...afraid you were going to follow in his footsteps. So I nagged at you to shape up. To rise above your gene pool. I should have talked less and listened more."

Noah shrugged. "Except that I wasn't saying anything. That's my fault."

"What did happen, Noah? Why did you suddenly turn from an A student to a . . . punk?"

"Remember when they arrested that boy in our class for pushing drugs?"

She frowned. "Yes. But what's that got to do with—"

"Everything."

"Oh, Noah, you weren't on drugs?"

He tossed his head. His fingertip traced the floral pattern on the sleeve of her hospital nightgown. "No. I was a narc."

"What!"

"Yeah. One time when we were having a cookout at your place, Chief Kapinski, except he wasn't police chief yet, got me aside and said he had a proposal for me. They needed someone to infiltrate the school and help them nail a heavy-duty drug pusher. At first I said no, but he said if I went undercover for him, the department would pick up the tab for my college education. My mother was a waitress, for crying out loud—I jumped at the chance."

Keely shook her head in confusion. "So all those times you got into trouble, you were really—"

"That's right. Setting up a phony pattern so I could get in with the rotten element at school. It was all a setup."

"Oh, Noah, why didn't you tell me? Did my father know?"

He nodded. "At least, I think he figured it out after a while. I didn't tell you because they told me not to trust anybody. But . . . somehow I expected you to use your crystal ball, I guess. But after you told me that you didn't want to see me anymore, I kind of freaked."

Keely felt her insides turn leaden as she recalled that last, horrible fight. Confused and shaken by Noah's sudden wildness, she had railed at him. She remembered with dreadful clarity telling him that he'd never amount to anything. That he was destined to become a nothing like his own father.

"So you kept it all bottled up inside?"

"Yeah. I was too stubborn to tell you then. I had this stupid idea that if you had faith in me, that you wouldn't have believed all those stories."

He broke off and stared into space. As memories flitted across his expressive face, she could see the hurt that still lingered.

Threading his fingers through his hair in a distracted gesture, he continued. "When I realized I'd lost your esteem, I guess I lost my own. It seemed better for everyone if I just went away. I couldn't bear to see the disappointment on your face any longer."

She blinked away the sudden stinging wetness behind her eyes. "Oh, Noah, I'm so sorry. So very sorry. If only I had known, but I should have trusted you."

"No! I understand now. You only tried to stop me from getting into more trouble. You did believe in me. Too bad I didn't believe in our relationship enough to trust you."

Suddenly, it all seemed so clear to him. He'd allowed his bitterness to color his life. Only one woman had the ability to soften him, to make him laugh. To make him whole.

Kneeling beside the bed, he took her hand in his. Staring into her wide, dark eyes, he found himself again. "Time's a pretty good teacher, I guess. I've been alone too long. Become harsh and bitter. But you've always been the one constant in my life, Keely. I loved you then and I love you now. Please don't tell me it's too late. Please say you love me.''

"Oh, Noah," she breathed, running her fingertips through the glorious texture of his hair. "I've never stopped loving you. But you have to promise me one thing."

"Anything."

She shook her head. "No, you have to promise. Say you'll never leave me again."

Noah shook his head as his lips at long last found those of his soul mate. He nuzzled the side of her neck and nibbled her earlobe. "Leave you? *No problema,* Keely. That'll never happen. We've got too much lost time to make up."

Keely cupped her hand behind his neck and drew him back to her. "Then we don't have a minute to waste, Bannister."

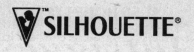

™ SILHOUETTE ®

Treat yourself to...

Wanted: Mother

Silhouette's annual tribute to motherhood takes a new twist in '97 as three sexy single men prepare for fatherhood and saying "I Do!"

Written by three captivating authors:

Annette Broadrick
Ginna Gray
Raye Morgan

Available: February 1997   Price: £4.99

COMING NEXT MONTH

THE IMPOSTOR
Cassie Miles

Avenging Angels

When Liz Carradine's boss was murdered, a sexy
detective appeared magically on her doorstep. In a
trench coat and fedora, Dash immediately won her
heart. Trouble was, he claimed to be an angel. Liz had
found the love of her life...but was he really going
back to heaven once he cracked the case?

MANHATTAN HEAT
Alice Orr

In twenty-four hours, a shocking murder and a man
named Memphis Modine changed Bennett St. Simon's
life forever! Memphis was dark and dangerous and
accused of a crime. But he shattered Bennett's
privileged existence, making her pulse race—and now
she was determined to prove his innocence!

COMING NEXT MONTH

STRANGER IN PARADISE
Amanda Stevens

Emily Townsend's life turned upside down the day
Matthew Steele blew into town. As she sized up the
stranger astride his Harley, she found herself lost in his
arresting grey eyes. Was it mere coincidence that
Matthew resembled the alleged killer from all those
years ago, or could he be her knight in shining black
leather?

PRINCE OF TIME
Rebecca York

43 Light Street

A devastating avalanche was the last thing Cassandra
Devereaux expected while hiking in the Alaskan
wilderness. Only by scrambling into a cave was she
able to survive. And when the cave was sealed by
snow and ice, Cassandra wasn't at all prepared for the
sight that awaited her deep in the underground lair...

COMING NEXT MONTH FROM

SILHOUETTE®

Sensation

A thrilling mix of passion, adventure and drama

DANGEROUS Lee Magner
SURVIVE THE NIGHT Marilyn Pappano
ANOTHER MAN'S WIFE Dallas Schulze
THE LITTLEST COWBOY Maggie Shayne

Special Edition

Satisfying romances packed with emotion

A BRIDE FOR JOHN Trisha Alexander
THE BLACK SHEEP'S BRIDE Christine Flynn
FULL-TIME FATHER Susan Mallery
JUST A FAMILY MAN Carolyn Seabaugh
A HOME FOR HANNAH Pat Warren
THE COWBOY AND HIS BABY Sherryl Woods

Desire

Provocative, sensual love stories for the woman of today

DON'T FENCE ME IN Kathleen Korbel
BABY FEVER Susan Crosby
COWBOY DREAMING Shawna Delacorte
BRIDE OF A THOUSAND DAYS Barbara McMahon
A GIFT FOR BABY Raye Morgan
EMMETT Diana Palmer

DANGEROUS LOVE
Catherine Lanigan

Richard Bartlow was a man people noticed. He was ruthless when he needed to be and sincere when he wanted. He was sexy, ambitious and charming. And he was dangerous.

All the females in Richard Bartlow's life—his wife, naive heiress Mary Grace Whittaker; the other woman, ad agency executive Alicia Carrel; and his mistress, New Age massage therapist Michelle Windsong—serve calculated purposes in his climb to success. Destined never to meet, the women are brought together with far-reaching consequences when Richard plots a final act of deceit to save himself from possible imprisonment and begin a new life.

"Lanigan succeeds in spinning a highly suspenseful, romantic tale."
—Publisher's Weekly

"As a storyteller, Catherine Lanigan is in a class by herself: unequalled and simply fabulous."
—Affaire de Coeur

MIRA®

'Happy' Greetings!

Would you like to win a year's supply of Silhouette® books? Well you can and they're free! Simply complete the competition below and send it to us by 31st July 1997. The first five correct entries picked after the closing date will each win a year's subscription to the Silhouette series of their choice. What could be easier?

ACSPPMTHYHARSI

_____ _____

TPHEEYPSARA

_____ _____

RAHIHPYBDYTAP

_____ _____

NHMYRTSPAAPNERUY

____ _____ _____

DYVLTEPYAANINSEPAH

_____ _____ _____

YAYPNAHPEREW

_____ ____ _____

DMHPYAHRYOSETPA

_____ _____ ____

VRHYPNARSAEYNPIA

_____ _____

Please turn over for details of how to enter ☞

How to enter...

There are eight jumbled up greetings overleaf, most of which you will probably hear at some point throughout the year. Each of the greetings is a 'happy' one, i.e. the word 'happy' is somewhere within it. All you have to do is identify each greeting and write your answers in the spaces provided. Good luck!

When you have unravelled each greeting don't forget to fill in your name and address in the space provided and tick the Silhouette® series you would like to receive if you are a winner. Then simply pop this page into an envelope (you don't even need a stamp) and post it today. Hurry—competition ends 31st July 1997.

Silhouette 'Happy' Greetings Competition
FREEPOST, Croydon, Surrey, CR9 3WZ

Please tick the series you would like to receive if you are a winner

Desire™ ❏   Sensation™ ❏   Intrigue™ ❏   Special Edition™ ❏

Are you a Reader Service Subscriber?   Yes ❏   No ❏

Ms/Mrs/Miss/Mr _____
                                              (BLOCK CAPS PLEASE)

Address _____

_____

_____ Postcode _____

(I am over 18 years of age)

One application per household. Competition open to residents of the UK and Ireland only.

You may be mailed with other offers from other reputable companies as a result of this application. If you would prefer not to receive such offers, please tick box. ❏

C7A

mps MAILING PREFERENCE SERVICE   **DMA**